W9-DGD-283

BATMAN
'66
VOL. 5

BATMAN '66 VOL. 5

Written by
JEFF PARKER
RAY FAWKES
GABE SORIA
LEE ALLRED

Art by
BRENT SCHOONOVER
GIANCARLO CARACUZZO
JON BOGDANOVE
LUKAS KETNER
TY TEMPLETON
JESSE HAMM
SCOTT KOWALCHUCK
DEAN HASPIEL
JONATHAN CASE
MICHAEL ALLRED

Colors by
KELLY FITZPATRICK FLAVIA CARACUZZO
ROBERTO FLORES OMAR ESTEVEZ TONY AVIÑA
SCOTT KOWALCHUCK ALLEN PASSALAQUA
JONATHAN CASE LAURA ALLRED

Letters by
WES ABBOTT

Cover Art & Original Series Covers by
MICHAEL & LAURA ALLRED

BATMAN created by BOB KANE with BILL FINGER

TABLE OF CONTENTS

BATMAN '66 VOL. 5
Published by DC Comics.

DC Comics, 2900 West Alameda Ave. Burbank, CA 91505
Printed by RR Donnelley, Salem, VA, USA. 4/8/16. First Printing.
ISBN: 978-1-4012-6105-4

Library of Congress Cataloging-in-Publication Data

Names: Parker, Jeff, 1966- author. | Fawkes, Ray, author. | Haspiel, Dean, illustrator. | Allred, Mike (Mike Dalton) illustrator.
Title: Batman '66. Volume 5 / Jeff Parker, Ray Fawkes, writers ; Dean Haspiel, Michael Allred, artists.
Description: Burbank, CA : DC Comics, [2016]
Identifiers: LCCN 2016006069 | ISBN 9781401261054 (hardback)
Subjects: LCSH: Graphic novels. | Superhero comic books, strips, etc. | BISAC: COMICS & GRAPHIC NOVELS / Superheroes.
Classification: LCC PN6728.B36 P376 2016 | DDC 741.5/973—dc23
LC record available at http://lccn.loc.gov/2016006069

ALL
RED

GRAHR!!!

AN URGENT RESPONSE TO A THREAT!
SKREEEEECH
WANTED
--TIRED OF HAVING MY BELOVED NIECE MARSHA PUT IN THAT UNCOMFORTABLE PRISON!
TONIGHT I WILL HAVE CYRUS RETURN TO DEAL WITH YOU, BATMAN!
IT'S STILL ON ALL THE BROADCASTS!
CYRUS...THAT WASN'T THE NAME OF MARSHA'S GRAND MOGUL, WAS IT?
NO, IT'S A MUCH MORE TROUBLING REFERENCE, ROBIN.
I LOOKED THROUGH MY QUEEN OF DIAMONDS FILE BEFORE WE LEFT THE BATCAVE.
"THE GROOVY GRAVE OF SOLOMON GRUNDY"
AS YOU KNOW, MARSHA USES HER AUNT'S POTIONS TO ROMANTICALLY ENTHRALL MILLIONAIRE HUSBANDS UNTIL THEY OUTLIVE THEIR USEFULNESS.
ONE OF HER RECENT CAPTURES WAS CYRUS GOLD, THE WEALTHY OLYMPIC WRESTLING CHAMPION.
WHAT'S TROUBLING IS WHERE HE IS NOW...
GOTHAM CEMETERY
...HERE.
Written by JEFF PARKER
Art by BRENT SCHOONOVER
Colors by KELLY FITZPATRICK
Lettered by WES ABBOTT
Cover by MICHAEL and LAURA ALLRED

HILDA, CEASE YOUR ARCANE CHEMISTRY AT ONCE!
THERE'S NO LAW AGAINST PAYING RESPECTS TO THE DEAD, HEROES.
AND THE LATE CYRUS HERE WAS VERY LOYAL TO MY NIECE, TAKEN FROM US TOO SOON.
HERE LIES CYRUS GOLD
MARSHA TOLD HIM TO WAIT OUTSIDE AND FORGOT ABOUT HIM-- DURING THE WINTER.
FROZE TO DEATH, POOR LAD.
I AM MORE CONCERNED BY THE LAWS OF NATURE BEING BROKEN.
IF YOU'RE GOING TO DO WHAT I SUSPECT, YOU *MUST* STOP!
FAH!
FFSSKS
SHHHH!
HOLY ANIMATION! SHE'S GOT US, BATMAN!
OH POO, THAT'S NOT WHAT I HAVE PLANNED FOR YOU, ELF.
I SUSPECT YOU'LL BE FREE IN MINUTES.
THEN YOU CAN FACE THE *TRUE* THREAT.

FIRST, AS ERE'S NO TIME IGGING, I OPEN ATH THROUGH THE SOIL...
...ABOUT 1.3 QUARTS OF FUMING SULFURIC ACID INTO THIS SOGGY GROUND SHOULD REACH THE COFFIN!
VSSHHH
SHE'S CRAZY!
STILL, YOU MUST APPRECIATE THE APPLICATION OF SCIENTIFIC METHOD, ROBIN.
SHE'S ASSESSED THE DENSITY OF THE GROUND, AND WHAT QUANTITY OF SO_3* WILL REACT WITH WATER TO REACH SIX FEET AND PENETRATE A CASKET LID.
*SO_3 = SULFUR TRIOXIDE.

ALL CHILD'S PLAY COMPARED TO THIS PART, BATMAN.
THEY BARRED ME FROM TEACHING FOR USING THIS KIND OF ANCIENT CHEMISTRY!

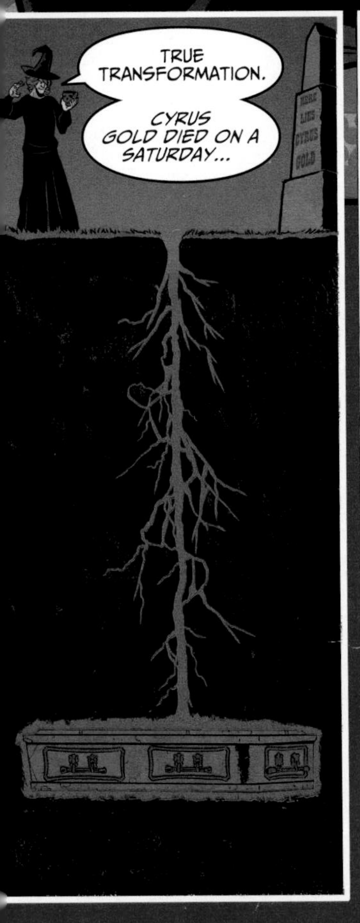

TRUE TRANSFORMATION.
CYRUS GOLD DIED ON A SATURDAY...

HIS POOR CURSED SOUL BURIED ON A SUNDAY...

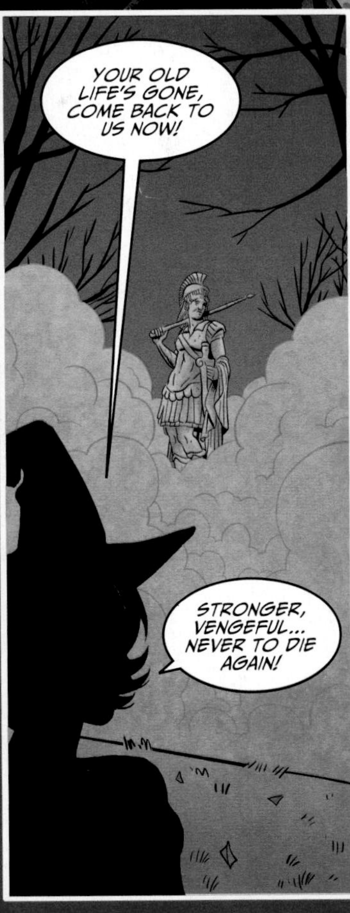

YOUR OLD LIFE'S GONE, COME BACK TO US NOW!
STRONGER, VENGEFUL... NEVER TO DIE AGAIN!

RISE THE NEW FORM...
...SOLOMON GRUNDY!!!
I... LIVE!!!!
HERE LIES

YES, DEAR! YOU DON'T HAVE TO WORRY ABOUT MARSHA OR ANY OF THE CONCERNS OF YOUR PAST LIFE.
YOU HAVE ONLY ONE REASON NOW TO WALK THE EARTH.

TO DESTROY BATMAN AND ROBIN!
KA-BOOOM!

YYYEESS...
...BAT... MAN...

GRUNDY **CRUSH** THE BAT MAN!
SCHLRUNK!!!
CHADWICK
RAAGHH!!!
KWHOOM!
HIS STRENGTH IS STAGGERING! WE'LL HAVE TO USE ALL OUR WITS!
HEE-HEEE! ALL IS SET IN MOTION, I'LL LISTEN TO THE GRISLY DETAILS OVER TEA BY THE RADIO!
AIIEEEEEEE
AFTER MURPHY
WELL. DRAT.

I'LL BRING DOWN THIS BRUTE!
HNNNH!
?
HEH HEH HEH HEH...
A CHOKEHOLD IS NO GOOD, ROBIN! GRUNDY DOESN'T NEED AIR!
WRONG... BAT... MAN...
CHOKE... WORK... FINE!
HLYRRRRKH--
HANG ON, LAD!
ROBBIN
WIN
APARO

SHWUNK!
ALL IMPACT--FOCUSED AT ONE POINT!
GRAHR!!!
PARKER
TRICK
NEXT TIME GRUNDY SQUEEZE HARD.
NEXT TIME GRUNDY CRUSH YOU!!!

RUN, BAT MAN, RUN! WILL DO YOU NO GOOD!
YOU HAVE TO STOP SOME TIME... REST. EAT.
SLEEP.
ADAMS
BUT GRUNDY KEEPS COMING, SEARCH-ING.
CAN'T ESCAPE... DEAD MAN WALKING.
ALLRED
HE'S RIGHT, BATMAN! HOW CAN WE STOP A VILLAIN WHO ISN'T EVEN ALIVE?
THE POWER OF THE BATMOBILE MAY HELP--WE CAN HIT HIM WITH THE BAT-BEAM!
YES, BAT MAN. HIT ME.

HIT ME... WITH EVERYTHING YOU'VE GOT!!!
HA HA HAAAA!!!
THE BATMOBILE... UPENDED!?!

BATMAN, THIS REALLY ISN'T GOING WELL!
CLEAR HEAD, CHUM! I THINK GRUNDY HAS GIVEN US THE CLUE WE NEED TO STOP HIM!

WE'LL NEED A LOT OF POWER...
...TO MAKE A DEAD MAN *LIVE.*

THE TRUNK IS OPEN. DISTRACT HIM FOR JUST A SECOND!
I'LL USE THIS!

CK, YOU GANTUAN HOUL!
TASTE DELICIOUS.

ANOTHER STIMULUS FOR YOU, GRUNDY!
NNNH?

GET CLEAR, ROBIN-- DON'T TOUCH HIM!
HA! BAT MAN THINK HE CAN HURT--

GR-R-R-UN N-N-N-DDD-YYYY!!
GOSH...YOU ELECTROCUTED HIM!
NO, I JUMPSTARTED HIS BODY, ROBIN--USING THE ATOMIC BATTERIES OF THE BATMOBILE AS A DEFIBRILLATOR!
I REASONED KICKING HIS BODY INTO HAVING A LIVING PERSON'S HEART RATE AND METABOLISM WOULD CONFLICT WITH HIS UNDEAD CHEMISTRY.
NOW WE'D BETTER GET HIM IN HEAVY CONTAINMENT BEFORE THE STASIS WEARS OFF!
I DON'T SUPPOSE YOU'D WANT TO HELP AN OLD WITCH OUT FIRST, WOULD YOU?
THE END

THE MARSHLANDS, MILES OUTSIDE GOTHAM CITY... A CHASE IS ON!
WWEEEEEEOOOOOOOOOOWWEEEEEEOO
HE MADE IT OUT, BATMAN!
HE WON'T GET FAR IN THESE MARSHES--COME ON!
HERE'S THE SERUM HE STOLE FROM THE LAB, JUST LIKE YOU PREDICTED HE WOULD...
...EMPTY!
ONCE THRONE LABS ANNOUNCED THEY WOULD ABANDON THE *FALSE FLESH* PROJECT AND DESTROY ALL THEIR SAMPLES, I SURMISED IT WOULD BRING OUR OLD ENEMY OUT OF HIDING.
I'VE TRIED TO PREPARE WELL FOR OUR ENCOUNTER TONIGHT.
FOR I'VE FINALLY PUT TOGETHER THE IDENTITY AND ORIGIN OF THE MAN FEARED BY THE LAW-ABIDING WORLD AS *FALSE FACE.*
"THE FINAL FORM"
Written by JEFF PARKER
Art by GIANCARLO CARACUZZO
Colors by FLAVIA CARACUZZO
Lettered by WES ABBOTT
Cover by MICHAEL and LAURA ALLRED

"HIS APPEARANCE IN GOTHAM FOLLOWS SOON AFTER THE *DISAPPEARANCE* OF THE CUNNING CRIMINAL KNOWN BY HIS TRUE NAME, *BASIL KARLO*.
"MY CASE STUDY POINTS TO ITS BEING KARLO WHO BROKE INTO THE LAB THREE YEARS AGO, AFTER THE FALSE FLESH/SYNTHETIC CELL PROJECT WAS ANNOUNCED.
"HE OFTEN SANDED OFF HI FINGERPRINTS TO AVOID LEAV EVIDENCE IN HIS CRIMES. NOW SAW A CHANCE TO CHANGE H IDENTITY COMPLETELY.
"A LAB ASSISTANT REPORTED THAT THE CRIMINAL DRANK THE SERUM...*NOT* HOW IT WAS INTENDED TO BE ADMINISTERED.
"IT WAS DESIGNED TO REVIVE DEAD SKIN CELLS--NECROTIC FLESH."
THE SERUM AFFECTED HIS ENTIRE CELLULAR STRUCTURE, MAKING IT HARD TO HOLD A CONSISTENT FORM FOR LONG.
ULTIMATELY, HE LOST NOT ONLY HIS IDENTITY, BUT ANY TRUE SENSE OF SELF. LOOK.
THE MASKS HE WEARS ARE MADE FROM A CAST OF HIS FACE BEFORE HE FORGOT HOW TO LOOK LIKE BASIL KARLO.
BEFORE BECAME THE WHO COUL *ANYONE*

BATMAN, THERE!
"AW, JUST THE SECURITY GUARD."
AH, BATMAN AND ROBIN! GOOD TO HAVE YOU OUT HERE.
SOMEONE BROKE INTO THRONE LABS-- I'M ON HIS TRAIL!
WE'RE EAGER TO HELP, SIR.
WE BELIEVE THE CRIMINAL TO BE THE FORM-SHIFTING MASTERMIND FALSE FACE.
REALLY? HE AVOIDED THE SAFE ENTIRELY.
HE WAS AFTER A SERUM!
SERUM? IS HE SELLING SECRET FORMULAS?
NO, I BELIEVE FALSE FACE WAS TRYING TO FIND AN INHIBITOR THAT WOULD STOP THE EFFECTS OF A PREVIOUS SERUM HE INGESTED.

UNFORTUNATELY, FALSE FACE CAN'T READ CHEMICAL NOTATION WELL.
WHAT HE STOLE WAS ACTUALLY A MORE REFINED COMPOUND OF WHAT HE DRANK BEFORE.
REALLY?

HIS BODY WOULD BE TRANSFORMING AS WE SPEAK.
IT WILL SOON BE INCREDIBLY DIFFICULT FOR HIM TO MAINTAIN A CONSISTENT FORM.

BUT I CAN STILL HOLD A GUN, DETECTIVE!
YOU NEED MEDICAL ATTENT FALSE FACE! I M ABLE TO NEUTRALI CHEMICALS IN YOUR IF YOU COME WIT BACK TO THE BATCAVE.
HOLY IMPOSTOR!
NICE TRY, BATS. I'M NOT FALLING FOR THAT ONE!
STOP!
AAHHH!!

IS...IS HE...?
ONE OF THE GREATEST PITFALLS OF THE MARSHLANDS...

SO FEW PEOPLE REALIZE WHAT A REAL AND EVER-PRESENT DANGER *QUICKSAND* IS IN OUR WORLD, ROBIN.
HOW STRUGGLING MAKES IT CLAIM THE VICTIM EVEN FASTE TO DRAG ONE DOWN TO ITS UNKNOWABLE DEPTHS.
GOS

I GUESS WE'VE FINALLY SEEN THE END OF FALSE FACE.
IRONIC THAT ONCE I FINALLY UNCOVERED HIS ORIGINS HE WOULD VANISH COMPLETELY.
PERHAPS I'LL PUT THIS MASK IN THE NEW DISPLAY WING OF THE BATCAVE...
...TO REMIND US OF THE EXCESSES OF THE VOLATILE CRIMINAL MIND.
IT COULD BE NEAR WHERE THE PENNY WILL GO.
OR NEAR THE ENORMOUS PLAYING CARD THAT HIGHLIGHTS THE JOKER'S DEPRAVED DEEDS.
THE HECK WITH THAT, BATMAN...
I WANT Y OWN WING F THE VILLAIN MUSEUM!
BUT DON'T CALL ME KARLO OR FALSE FACE IN THOSE PLACARDS.
I'M MORE THAN A MAN NOW, BATMAN. I'M AN ELEMENT OF THE EARTH ITSELF.
CALL ME...
...CLAYFACE!!!

YOUR BODY HAS BEEN DRASTICALLY ALTERED--WE NEED TO GET YOU HELP!
I KNOW. IT'S **BETTER** THAN BEFORE! ALL THAT GUNK IN THE QUICKSAND ADDED TO ME.

I HAVE A LOT MORE TO WORK WITH NOW, BATMAN.
INCREDIBLE!

NO MORE OF YOU FIGURING OUT WHO I AM, THEN PUNCHING MY LIGHTS OUT.
WELL, I MEAN, THERE STILL WILL BE A PUNCH-OUT.
YOU!

SLERCH!
AW, COME ON, CAPED CRUSADER. TRYING TO GIVE ME A HEADACHE?
OH, *THERE'S* THE BOY WONDER, RIGHT WHERE I WANT HIM.
SLORCH
I'M STUCK!
HERE-- WE NEED TO FORM A PLAN OF ATTACK!
WHEW!
POP!
CLAYFACE IS CLEARLY POWERFUL AND DANGEROUS.
WE NEED TO USE OUR ADVANTAGE OF NUMBERS AND KEEP HIS ATTENTION SPLIT.
OKAY, I'LL RUN AROUND BEHIND HIM!
BLOOP!
SORRY, BOYS, BUT I KEPT AN EAR OUT FOR YOU AND KNOW YOUR PLAN.
KEEPING MY ATTENTION SPLIT *WON'T* WORK.

YOU DON'T REALIZE HOW MUCH I'VE CHANGED...
IT'S EASY FOR ME TO DIVIDE MY FOCUS NOW!
HOLY HALFSIES!
LET'S MAKE A REALLY FAIR FIGHT...
...SHALL WE?
COME MEET YOUR MATCH!
HA HA HAAA HAAA!!
CL-POW!!
CL-THUMP!
HAVE...NO CHOICE.

RE'S
SCAPE,
MAN.
NOT FROM YOURSELF!
IM...POSSIBLE! YOU CAN'T MAKE EVEN MORE!
NOTHING IS IMPOSSIBLE WITH ME NOW!
I DON'T NEED HENCHMEN ANYMORE EITHER.
I'M A ONE-MAN GANG!
NOW IT'S TIME FOR YOU TWO TO VISIT THE QUICKSAND PIT BACK THERE.
EXCEPT YOU WON'T BE COMING BACK OUT.
WIN,
FACE...
YOU
YOUR
NTITY.
WHILE I STILL HAVE MINE, SOMETHING YOU CAN NEVER TAKE AWAY!
OH, I WOULDN'T SAY THAT.
I'LL GET THE HANG OF SHAPING THIS FORM JUST LIKE I DID BEFORE.
IN NO TIME I'LL BE ABLE TO BE A PERFECT REPLICA OF ANYONE ON EARTH.
NOT ME! I'M THE ONE PERSON YOU CAN NEVER BE NOW, CLAYFACE.
GO AHEAD, LOOK!

HA, I'LL...
...NO...
NO!
THAT'S RIGHT, CLAYFACE. I'M BASIL KARLO, THE MAN YOU *USED* TO BE.
AND NOW YOU'RE *NOBODY*. JUST A BUNCH OF *CHEAP CLAY COPIES*.
NOOOOO!!!
THEY'RE ALL CATATONIC! BATMAN, WHAT HAPPENED?
MY THEORY? HE SPREAD HIMSELF TOO THIN, ROBIN.
MY PREPARATION WAS INTENDED TO CONFUSE DESPERATE FALSE FACE IN CASE NEEDED AN ACE-IN-THE-HOLE FOR DISTRACTION.
BUT WITH HIS MIND FRAGMENTED SO THOROUGHLY, CLAYFACE COULDN'T DEAL WITH SUCH A CONTRADICTORY PIECE OF INFORMATION.
IN SHORT, HE-- OR THEY-- SUFFER FROM...
...AN EXISTENTIAL CRISIS.

ALL
RED

ZLONK!
POW!!!

"DIAMOND DISASTER"
Written by RAY FAWKES Art by JON BOGDANOVE
Colors by ROBERTO FLORES and OMAR ESTEVEZ
red by WES ABBOTT Cover by MICHAEL and LAURA ALLRED
BUSINESS AS USUAL AT THE FIRST BANK OF GOTHAM... ...OR IS IT?
FIRST BANK OF GOTHAM
I WANT IT ALL! EVERY PENNY!
ITHDRAW IT ALL!
I WANT IT OUT!
EVERY LAST RED CENT!
THEY'VE ALL GONE MAD!
GET ME THE POLICE!

NDERSTAND, MISTER CKSLEY. YES, IT DOES EEM STRANGE THAT MANY MILLIONAIRES OULD BE EMPTYING THEIR ACCOUNTS AT ONCE.
BUT IT'S NO CRIME!
BEGORRAH! WE'VE BEEN TAKING FUNNY CALLS LIKE THIS ALL MORNING!
CHIEF
AT THIS RATE, ALL THE VAULTS IN GOTHAM WILL BE EMPTIER THAN A--
RIGHT YOU ARE, CHIEF...
...SO WE'D BEST MAKE A CALL OF OUR OWN.

I UNDERSTAND, COMMISSIONER.
BATMAN AND ROBIN ARE *ON THE CASE.*
TO THE BATPOLES!
BUT, SIR!
YOU'RE SCHEDULED TO APPEAR AT THE CHARITY B THE GOTHAM MUSEUM'S DIAMOND GALA TO BENEFIT--
DICK

--WAYWARD YOUTH.
YES, OF COURSE.
HOLY OBLIGATIONS! WHAT DO WE *DO?*
HMM. SOMETIMES AN OBLIGATION CAN BECOME AN *OPPORTUNITY.*
MOST OF THE GUESTS AT THE GALA ARE GOING TO BE THE SAME *MILLIONAIRES* WHO WERE AT THE BANK TODAY.
MAYBE WE CAN DO SOME INVESTIGATING *AT* THE GALA!
DICK
EXACTLY RIGHT.
I SENSE A SUBTLE SKILL AT WORK HERE, OLD CHUM. WE MAY FIND OURSELVES IN *NEFARIOUS* COMPANY.
WHO DO YOU THINK WE'LL MEET? THE JOKER? THE RIDDLER?
I DON'T KNOW.
THERE'S ONLY ONE WAY TO FIND OUT. COME ON!

E GOTHAM CITY MUSEUM...
EYES OPEN, CHUM. THIS ENCHANTING DISPLAY MAY CONCEAL OUR FOE.
REMEMBER, THE BATMOBILE IS HIDDEN IN THE BUSHES JUST OUTSIDE THE DOOR--JUST IN CASE.
TO BENEFIT WAYWARD YOUTH
WOW.
LOOK AT THAT!
THEY'RE ALL THROWING THEIR OWN JEWELRY ON THE PILE! EVEN COMMISSIONER GORDON!
THIS IS EITHER THE MOST SUCCESSFUL CHARITY BALL I'VE EVER SEEN...
...OR THE MOST DIABOLICAL ROBBERY!

YOU DON'T MEAN--
YES!
MIND CONTROL!
WELCOME! NOW...COME TO ME...
...MY DARLINGS...

Behold!

OOOOH...
...SO SHINY...
NO! LOOK AWAY!

DONATIONS FOR HER HIGHNESS. DIAMONDS ARE PREFERRED.
I'VE GOT SOME MONEY SOMEWHERE...
DIAMONDS? HER HIGHNESS?
I SHOULD'VE KNOWN! IT'S...

MARSHA, QUEEN OF DIAMONDS!
YES, MY DARLINGS!
TAKE IT ALL! EVERY PENNY!
TEN DOLLARS. VERY GOOD, SIR.
THIS IS NO PLACE FOR BRUCE WAYNE...
IT'S A GOOD THING I HAD ALFRED HIDE THE BATMOBILE NEARBY!
HANG ON, OLD CHUM! I'LL BE RIGHT BACK!

BATMAN!
WHO INVITED YOU?
PASTE HIM!
YES, YOUR HIGHNESS!
WHAP!
I'LL PULVERIZE HIM, MY QUEEN!
NOT TODAY!
POW!!
MARSHA!
PAF!

BASH!
HOW RUDE!

WHACK!
EEEYOW!

WHAM!
NO, MARSHA! DON'T LEAVE! TAKE MY MONEY!
TAKE IT ALL!

STOP RIGHT THERE!
THIS GALA WAS SUPPOSED TO BENEFIT WAYWARD YOUTHS!
ARE YOU SAYING I'M NOT A YOUTH?
BATMAN, HOW COULD YOU?

SLAM!
CLICK!

SLAM!
LOCKED!

TOODLE-OO, DARLING!
YOU WON'T
ET AWAY THIS
ME, MARSHA!
NO PARKING ANY TIME
GOTHAM CIT
MUSEUM PA
READY AND WAITING, EH, ROBIN?
NO TIME TO WASTE!
WE HAVE TO CATCH UP TO HER!
VAROOM!

SHE WON'T GET AWAY!

WAIT FOR US, MARSHA!
I HAVE TO GIVE HER THIS PRESENT!
THE BATMOBILE'S DIAMOND-STUDDED BRAKES!
EMERGENCY BAT-TURN LEVER
I KNOW MARSHA WILL LOVE THESE.
YOU'RE STILL IN A TRANCE!
BUT IF YOU'VE GOT THE BRAKES...
THE BATMOBILE CAN'T STOP!
VROOM!!

RED LIGHT!
YIELD
AMBULANCE!
MISTER FROSTY!
OH, NO!

EEEEEE!
THE BATMOBILE IS OUT OF CONTROL!
STOP
KABOOM

PHEW!
CHALK THIS LUCKY ESCAPE UP TO QUICK REFLEXES AND A STURDY BAT-ROPE, EH, CHUM?
MARSHA...?
ROBIN!
YOU'VE BEEN HYPNOTIZED!
CAN YOU HEAR ME?

LATER, IN THE BATCAVE...
THANKS FOR PICKING US UP ON THE ROAD, ALFRED. WE'D HAVE BEEN IN FOR QUITE A WALK WITHOUT THE BATMOBILE...
OF COURSE, SIR. BUT DO YOU THINK WE CAN FREE ROBIN FROM MARSHA'S MIND CONTROL?
WE MUST TRY.
HIS TRANCE STATE WAS CAUSED BY THE LIGHTS SHE WAS SHINING AT THE CHARITY BALL.
GOGGLES ON, ALFRED. IF I CAN PROGRAM THE BAT-COMPUTER TO CREATE A PATTERN OF INTERFERENCE...
IT JUST...
...MIGHT...

...FREE HIS MIND!
MARSHA?

HMM.
NOT QUITE, SIR.
TRY, TRY AGAIN. FIVE HUNDRED MILLICYCLES, THIS TIME!

MARSHA?

TWO THOUSAND MILLICYCLES!
MARSHA?

FOUR THOUSAND MILLICYCLES!
MARSHA?

EIGHT THOUSAND MILLICYCLES!
BATMAN!
AHA!

NO TIME TO WASTE, ROBIN!
IT'S TIME TO PUT MARSHA OUT OF BUSINESS!
Gotham City
14 MILES

WHY DON'T WE TAKE THE BATMOBILE?
IT'S OUT OF COMMISSION!
I'LL EXPLAIN LATER!

HERE'S OUR RIDE!
GOTHAM'S *FINEST* PUBLIC TRANSIT.
BUS STOP
TO CITY
I HOPE I HAVE EXACT *CHANGE*...

WHAT'S THE PLAN, BATMAN?
WHERE ARE WE HEADED?
THE COMMISSIONER'S HOUSE.

I JUST HOPE WE'RE NOT TOO *LATE*...
DON'T WORRY, BATMAN. I'LL GET YOU THERE AS QUICK AS I CAN!
THANK YOU, DRIVER.
BUT PLEASE MAINTAIN A SAFE DRIVING SPEED.
HOLY URBAN TRAFFIC!

AND SOON...
THERE'S THE COMMISSIONER! GOOD THING HE'S HOME!
BUT HE'S JUST LEAVING!

MARSHA...
QUICK, ROBIN!
HITCH A RIDE!

BUT WHERE ARE WE GOING NOW, BATMAN?

"IF MY HUNCH IS CORRECT...
Sparkling Star
Hotel
"...STRAIGHT TO MARSHA'S HIDEOUT!"

AH! COMMISSIONER GORDON, DARLING!
HAVE YOU BROUGHT ME A GIFT?

YES, MY BEAUTY!
ALL I HAVE!

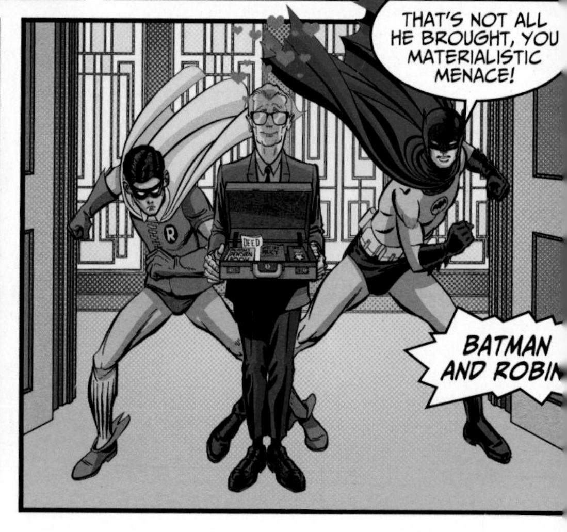
THAT'S NOT ALL HE BROUGHT, YOU MATERIALISTIC MENACE!
BATMAN AND ROBIN

WAIT!
NO NEED TO FIGHT...
...WHEN YOU CAN SEE MY LOVELY LIGHT!
MARSHA...
OH, MARSHA...
YES! THEY'RE MINE!
NOW THAT I HAVE YOU UNDER MY SPELL, DARLING...
WHAT SHALL I DO WITH YOU?

NOW, ROBIN!
WHAT?

ZAP!!!
NO!
BUT... HOW?

ONCE WE KNEW THE FREQUENCY OF YOUR HYPNO-SPARKLES, IT WAS A SIMPLE THING TO TIME OUR BLINKING TO KEEP OUT THE LIGHT.
IMPOSSIBLE, DARLING!
NOTHING IS IMPOSSIBLE WHEN YOU KEEP TO A HIGH STANDARD OF SELF-DISCIPLINE, MARSHA.
LOOK OUT, BATMAN!

OOOOFF!
WHACK!
SLAM!
WHAM!

ONK!
POW!!

POW!!
BIFF
BOFF!
SPLATT!
KLONK

Z-ZWAP!

I GUESS WE'RE DONE HERE!
NOT QUITE YET, ROBIN...
TAP! TAP!

MARSHA?
WE STILL HAVE TO FREE THE COMMISSIONER...
...AND ALL THE OTHER PEOPLE UNDER MARSHA'S SPELL.

OF COURSE! BUT HOW!

THE SAME WAY I FREED YOU, ROBIN.
WE'LL JUST HAVE TO MAKE A FEW ADJUSTMENTS TO MARSHA'S MACHINE...

BATMAN! ROBIN!
WHAT'S GOING ON HERE?
ANOTHER ONE OF MARSHA'S DEVILISH PLANS, COMMISSIONER.
BUT WE'VE *NEUTRALIZED* THE EFFECTS, AND IT'S TIME TO PUT THE DISHONEST DEBUTANTE BEHIND BARS.
HOW *BORING!*
NOT *QUITE*, YOUNG LADY...

...THERE'S NOTHING MORE EXCITING THAN *JUSTICE!*
WELL SAID, COMMISSIONER!

YOU HAVEN'T SEEN THE LAST OF ME, DYNAMIC DUO!
BY ALL THAT SHINES AND SPARKLES, I *SWEAR* IT!

YOU THINK SHE'LL REALLY BE BACK, BATMAN?
I WOULDN'T DOUBT IT, ROBIN.
MARSHA IS A WOMAN OF MANY *WILES.*
BUT IF SHE DOES RETURN TO MENACE GOTHAM...
...WE WILL *ALWAYS* BE THERE!
WIELDING THE ONL
THING *HARDER* THA
DIAMOND...
...THE
EVEN-HAND
RESOLV
OF DECE
CITIZENS
THE

AT'S THIS?
URGLED BAKERY?
TECTORS OF PEACE,
TED WITH PIES???
THE ENTIRE BAKERY IS BOOBY-TRAPPED, ROBIN!
HMMGHLF!

"NIGHT OF THE HARLEQUIN"

Written by JEFF PARKER Art by LUKAS KETNER Colors by KELLY FITZPATRICK
Lettered by WES ABBOTT Cover by MICHAEL and LAURA ALLRED

INK
S ALL
HEM!
I'M SORRY, BATMAN, I TRY TO WARN YOU!
SKLRCH
I RUSH IN WHEN I HEAR CASH REGISTER OPEN, AND *THOK!* I SEE STARS.

DID YOU SEE WHO BROKE IN, MR. LUCENZI?
NO! TOO DARK, BUT I HEARD... A LADY'S LAUGH.
THE PERPETRATOR LEFT A CLUE.

I THINK WE KNOW WHERE TO START.

WELL, NOW, I'D BE *FIBBING* IF I SAID THIS CALLING CARD WASN'T FAMILIAR.
AT THE ARKHAM INSTITUTE...
BUT YOU CAN ASK ALL THE DOCTORS, I'VE NOT LEFT THE PREMISES.
HEH HEH HEH
SEEMS I HAVE SOME FANS CARRYING ON MY GOOD WORK. THE PIES WERE SPRING-LOADED, YOU SAY?
I'M A *CAKE* MAN, M'SELF.
THIS IS RAISING A LONG-HELD CONCERN OF MINE.
DR. HUGO, ARE YOU STILL TREATING YOUR FORMER ASSOCIATE, DR. HOLLY QUINN?
I AM. SHE'S BEEN VERY CALM OF LATE, I HOPE THAT WE'RE MAKING PROGRESS.
HER MENTAL STRAIN FROM UNDOING THE EFFECTS OF *THE JOKER WAVE* SEEMED IRREVERSIBLE...
...BUT HER HYSTER HAS ABATE LATELY.
HMM.

HEE HEE HEE HEE HA HA!
SHE SEEMS TO BE IN A GOOD MOOD.
NO...
...THAT'S NOT HOLLY QUINN'S VOICE!

HEE HEE HEE HAA HAAA--
--HI, OSSIFERS...
THAT'S NURSE FITZ!
B+R
NO2
SHE'S BEEN BREATHING NITROUS OXIDE...LAUGHING GAS!
HOO HOO... HAHA--HOLLY LEFT A NOTEY-NOTE...HEE...
"Nurse Fitz is a lot of laughs, isn't she? Sorry I couldn't stick around, I have a new career to pursue. Tell Joker I'll make him proud! Tee-hee!
"Signed... Harlequin."

IT'S WORSE THAN I FEARED. THAT POOR WOMAN'S MIND WAS PUSHED OVER THE EDGE.
SHE *SACRIFICED* HER SANITY SO THAT THE GOOD PEOPLE OF GOTHAM COULD KEEP THEIRS.

WITH HER YEARS OF STUDY AND DEPTH OF KNOWLEDGE, SHE MAY BE MORE DANGEROUS THAN THE JOKER EVER WAS!
YOU COULD HAVE WAITED TO SAY THAT OUTSIDE!

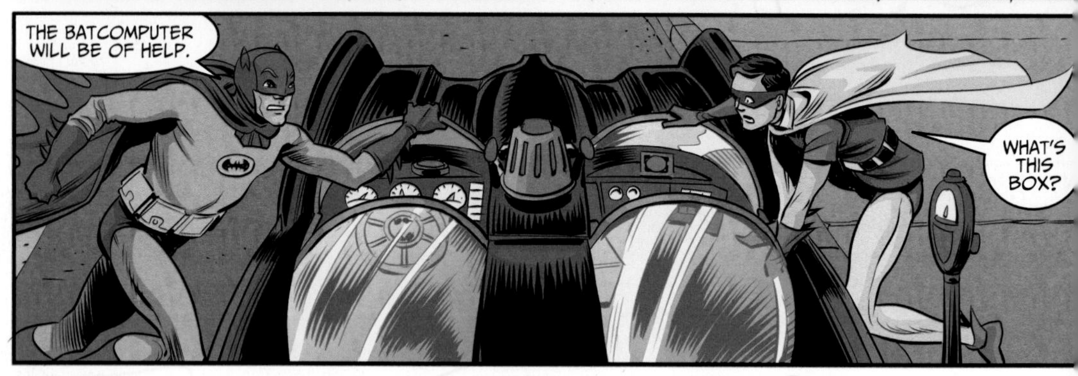
THE BATCOMPUTER WILL BE OF HELP.
WHAT'S THIS BOX?

THAT WASN'T THERE BEFORE!

UH...
BOING
SPROING

HOLY REJECTION!
EJECTED FROM OUR OWN BATMOBILE!
OOF!
TO ASSESS THE CONTROLS AND PLACE A TRIGGERING DEVICE THAT QUICKLY TAKES AN ADVANCED MIND WITH A WARPED SENSE OF HUMOR...
...READY YOURSELF, ROBIN. WE ARE CERTAINLY ABOUT TO ENCOUNTER THIS NEW VILLAIN...
...THE HARLEQUIN!!!
HI, HEROES! JUST WHERE YOU'D EXPECT A BAT AND A BIRD TO BE, HUH?
GOLLY, IT'S A REAL HONOR THAT YOU CAME ALL THE WAY OUT HERE TO WELCOME ME TO YOUR GALLERY OF ROGUES!
I PROMISE TO DO MY BEST TO LIVE UP TO YOUR HIGH STANDARD OF VILLAINY AND COME UP WITH SOME NEAT SCHTICK THAT MAKES CHASING ME AROUND GOTHAM EXTRA FUN!
HYUCK

MISS QUINN, YOU NEED TO RETURN TO PSYCHIATRIC CARE...
OH, FOO! I USED TO *BE* ONE OF THOSE DOCTORS, BATMAN!
WE JUST DAYDREAM WHILE WE LISTEN TO THE PATIENTS AND TELL THEM TO PRETEND THEY'RE *KIDS* AGAIN.
NOW I GOTTA GO GET BACK TO MY CRIME SPREE, I JUST WANTED TO SAY HI IN PERSON.
'CAUSE COMMISSIONER GORDON WON'T BE ABLE TO CALL YOU AND TELL YOU WHERE I'VE BEEN REPORTED!
THE HOTLINE TO THE BATPHONE!
SSSSSRRSH
SO LONG, DREAMBOAT--I M
DREAM*BAT.*
HARLEQUIN IS GETTING AWAY!
MUST...
...PUNCTURE...
...BALLOON...!
HEY! DO YOU KNOW HOW MUCH ONE OF THESE BALLOONS *COSTS?!*
IF YOU FIND OUT, TELL ME, BECAUSE I *STOLE* THIS ONE!
AND I'M GONNA DO A LOT MORE OF THAT NOW, BROTHER.
SEE YA IN THE FUNNY PAPERS, *CAPED CRYBABIES!*

RAAPPP!
HAR!
MAYOR
HOO!
YUM!
LOOK OUT!
MADNESS AND MAYHEM
DESCEND UPON GOTHAM CITY!
WHEE!
HOLY CLOWN PRINCESS OF CRIME!
TEE HEE!
BAT-PHONE
OH NO!
CAN NOTHING STOP
THIS ONE-WOMAN
CRIMEWAVE?!?
COMPLETE... AND UTTER...
...CHAOS!
BANG

ONE NIGHT, DOWN IN THE WAREHOUSE DISTRICT...
THANKS, EVERYONE WHO ANSWERED MY WHISPERED MESSAGES TO THE CRIMINAL UNDERWORLD!
AND TO THOSE OF YOU WHO JUST LIKE HANGING OUT IN OLD WAREHOUSES.
AS YOU KNOW, I'VE SPENT THE PAST TWO WEEKS INTRODUCING MYSELF TO GOTHAM.
SO NOW EVERYBODY KNOWS THE NAME HARLEQUIN, EVEN IF THEY DON'T SPELL IT SO GOOD. IT'S TIME TO PROGRESS AS A VILLAIN.
FOR INSTANCE, ALL THIS CRIME AND CRAZINESS IS A LOT OF WORK--I'M POOPED!
SO I THOUGHT TO MYSELF--WHAT WOULD JOKER DO?
ANSWER--HE'D HIRE SOME HENCHMEN! GOONS! LACKEYS!
YOU GUYS! I'VE GOT BIG IDEAS, AND MONEY, YOU'VE GOT CRAGGY FACES AND KNUCKLES--LET'S MAKE THIS HAPPEN!
ME!
I'M YER MAN!
NO, I'M THE TOUGHEST, HIRE ME!

WOW, THIS IS TOUGH. I COULD JUST HIRE ALL OF YOU AND HAVE A SMALL ARMY, BUT THEN MY HARD-STOLEN MONEY WOULDN'T GO FAR.
HMM...
I GOT AN IDEAR, MISS.
I SAYS WE ALL DUKE IT OUT! DA LAST FIVE GUYS STANDIN' ARE DA BEST, AND DAT'S YER GANG.
OH, YEAH?!
YAYYY! I CAN ALREADY TELL YOU'RE GOING TO BE A GOOD LACKEY!
ALL RIGHT, BOYS, IN IT TO WIN IT!
I NEED SELF-STARTERS! SHOW ME YOUR RESUMES...
...FIGHT!
WHAT WOULD YOU SAY IS YOUR GREATEST WEAKNESS?
WHAM!
OOOFF!
UNK!!
SOMETIMES, I JUST WANNA SLUG EVERYBODY!
POWIE!!!

B-WHAM!
WAIT, WAAIIIT! I NEEDED FIVE LEGBREAKERS, DIAL IT DOWN!
NOW THERE'S ONLY TWO!
SORRY MISS HARLE WE JUST RE WANTED T JOB!

OH, WELL--AT LEAST YOU ALREADY HAVE A MASK LIKE I WANTED.
YOU DIDN'T BRING A CLOWN NOSE AND LABELED SHIRT, DID YOU?
I GOT SOMETHIN' IN HERE THAT MIGHT FILL DA BILL.

WHAT CAN I CALL YOU GUYS... JESTERS? BOZOS?
IS THAT A CAPE YOU'RE PUTTING ON, BOZO-1?

IT IS, HARLEQUIN. IN THE FUTURE, YOU MIGHT WANT TO REMEMBER THAT WE'RE MASTERS OF DISGUISE.
YOU'RE UNDER ARREST!
I CAN'T BELIEVE IT-- AGGGH!
JUST TELL ME ONE THING--
--HOW WAS I? CATWOMAN-LEVEL? EGGHEAD?
DEFINITELY GETTING THERE!

MONDAY MORNING IN GOTHAM CITY, AND WORKERS ARE STARTING ANOTHER EEK OF HONEST TOIL...
...INCLUDING BARBARA GORDON, AKA BATGIRL--
--BEGINNING HER FIRST DAY AT A TEMPORARY JOB.
ONE THREE SEVEN
HOLD THAT ELEVATOR, MY GOOD MAN!
23RD FLOOR. EXPRESS!
YES, SIR!
F.K.R.&D. ADVERTISING
F.K.R.&D. ADVERTISING
F.K.R.&D. ADVERTISING
23RD FLOOR, FKR&D ADVERTISING!
CAN YOU INFORM YOUR SUPERIOR THAT HIS TEN O'CLOCK IS HERE?
TEN? THERE'S NOTHING IN HIS BOOK UNTIL LUNCH. I'M AFRAID YOU MUST BE MISTAKEN, MISTER...?

COBBLEPOT, MY DEAR! OSWALD C! AND ASSOCIATES. CLEAR EVERYONE'S SCHEDULES...
WRITTEN BY GABE SORIA
ART BY TY TEMPLETON
COLORS BY TONY AVIÑA
LETTERED BY WES ABBOTT
BATMAN '66 PRESENTS PENGUIN, CATWOMAN, JOKER, RID AND BARBARA GORDON IN...
...WE'RE YOUR NEW CLIENTS! WAUGH!
BADMEN

RIDDLE ME THIS, MEN AND WOMEN IN GREY FLANNEL SUITS--WHY HAVE GOTHAM CITY'S MOST NOTORIOUS VILLAINS TAKEN THE ENTIRE STAFF OF ITS MOST PRESTIGIOUS AD AGENCY HOSTAGE?
LET ME HAZARD A GUESS-- A HANDSOME RANSOM? NO WORRIES ABOUT THAT. BETWEEN THE SENIOR PARTNERS HERE, WE'VE GOT ENOUGH MONEY TO KEEP YOU JOKERS-- NO OFFENSE, JOKER-- IN DEATH TRAPS UNTIL 1975.

YOU WOULD THINK THAT, BUT OW WRONG YOU ARE! WHAT WE REQUIRE IS SOMETHING MUCH MORE EPHEMERAL IN NATURE!
WE NEED TO RESURRRRRECT OUR IMAGES.
ANSWER-- BAD PUBLICITY IS KILLING US AND WE NEED A MALICIOUS *MAKEOVER!*
GOTHAM CITY SHOULD LOVE TO *HATE* US AS MUCH AS WE LOVE *STEALING* FROM IT!
AND THE SUREST WAY TO CONVINCE THE *HOI POLLOI* IS WITH *ADVERTISING.*

THIS AGENCY'S VARD-WINNING K FOR CHEMICAL MPANIES, ARMS FACTURERS, AND IER INDUSTRIES R AND DEAR TO JR HEARTS, IS PERFECT FIT FOR US.
ARMSCO. HELPS PUPPIES!
GLEEMONEX puts a SMILE on your face!!

SO WHO WANTS TO HELP US REBRAND?
SO THAT'S THEIR SCHE[ME] IF ONLY I HA[D] BATGIRL COS[TUME] WITH ME...
...I COULD MAKE A QUICK CHANGE OUT OF MY WORK CLOTHES...
STORAGE ROOM
...INTO MY WORK CLOTHES!
THEN I'D GET THE DROP ON THESE KOOKY CROOKS.
I CALL THIS MEETING TO ORDER... LAW AND ORDER, THAT IS!
BATGIRL!

BAD KITTY!
SOCK!
HOW'S THAT FOR A PUNCHLINE?
POW!!
WHEN IT RAINS IT POURS, PENGUIN!

BUT I DON'T
AVE MY COSTUME
R MY UTILITY BELT
WITH ME. SO I
UPPOSE IF I CAN'T
BEAT THEM...
...I'LL JOIN THEM!
I VOLUNTEER! I'LL HELP THE VILLAINS OF GOTHAM CITY!
I SENSE A PROMOTION IN YOUR FUTURE, MY DEAR!
WHAT'S THIS? BARBARA GORDON--BATGIRL--IS GOING TO HELP THIS ROGUES GALLERY WIN THE HEARTS AND MINDS OF GOTHAM CITY?
UNBELIEVABLE!

AND THE EXECUTIVES AT FKR&D CAN'T BELIEVE IT EITHER, BUT FOR DIFFERENT REASONS.
YOU CAN'T HIRE HER TO HEAD YOUR CAMPAIGN-- SHE'S A TEMP, FOR CRYIN' OUT LOUD!
HOW ABOUT WE GO OUT FOR A THREE-HOUR LUNCH AND DISCUSS THIS OVER DRINKS? WE'LL EXPENSE IT. WHAT'S YOUR POISON?
THREE HOURS?!
WAUGH!
HOW DO YOU PEOPLE EVER GET ANY WORK DONE AROUND HERE? CRIME TAKES TIME! EFFORT! INDUSTRY!
"CRIME TAKES TIME"-- THAT'S REMARKABLE. YOU'RE A NATURAL, PENGUIN!
THANK YOU.

NOW, MISS...?
BARBARA.
...MISS BARBARA, HERE, SHE'S SHOWN INITIATIVE! ESSENTIAL FOR GETTING AHEAD IN THIS HARSH WORLD. SHE'S RUNNING THE SHOW.
THE REST OF YOU GET LOCKED IN THE BREAK ROOM-- LET'S GET TO WORK!

HOURS LATER, THE TEAM HAS REACHED A CREATIVE IMPASSE...
EUREKA! I'VE GOT IT! CATWOMAN-- TAKE A MEMO!
I TRUST THAT WAS A JOKE, HMMMMM?
ER, OF COURSE, MY DEAR. WORKPLACE JOCULARITY! NO NEED TO TAKE THIS TO HUMAN RESOURCES.

NINE-TO-FIVE IS SO DULL. T'S GO ROB A BANK!
RIDDLE ME THIS--WHEN'S QUITTING TIME?
PERHAPS INSPIRATION WILL STRIKE IF WE MAKE THIS AGENCY OUR OWN. GIVE IT A NEW NAME!
I HUMBLY SUBMIT... PJR&C. IT'S BOLD. SIMPLE. STARTS WITH "P." WHAT SAY YOU, MY FELLOW CROOKED CREATIVES?

HOW ABOUT JRC&P?
RIDDLE ME THIS, JOKER-- SHOULDN'T IT BE RCP&J?

PURRRRSONALLY, I'D PREFER CPJ&R.
PJR&C!

JRC&P!
CPJ&R!
RCP&J!
PJR&C!
THAT'S IT!
THEY'VE GIVEN ME AN IDEA FOR HOW TO HALT THIS HOSTILE TAKEOVER. NOW TO PUT THIS PLAN IN MOTION...
STOP! I THINK I'VE GOT IT!

SO SOON, AFTER A CONSULTATION WITH ONE OF THE AGENCY'S TOP ARTISTS, BARBARA IS READY TO MAKE HER PRESENTATION...
TO BEGIN WITH, LET'S FACE THE FACTS-- GOTHAM CITY IS BORED OF YOU.
BORED? OF THE JOKER? BUT I'M THE CLOWN PRINCE OF CRIME. I'M VERY ENTERTAINING!
QUIET! LET HER TALK.
YOU'VE ALL BECOME OLD HAT. ON MONDAY, CATWOMAN HEISTS A PET SHOW. TUESDAY, THE RIDDLER ROBS A MUSEUM, WEDNESDAY...WELL, YOU GET THE IDEA.
THEY'RE TAKING US FOR GRANTED.
EXACTLY! YOU NEED TO SHAKE THINGS UP. AND THEN THE ANSWER HIT ME. ACTUALLY, YOU WALKED IN WITH THE IDEA, PENGUIN.
I DID?
I GOT JESSICA HERE FROM THE ART DEPARTMENT TO HELP ME WHIP THIS CONCEPT TOGETHER.
IT'S NOT FINAL, BUT I THINK WE'VE GOT IT.
LADY AND GENTLEMEN, MAY WE PRESENT TO YOU...

PENGUIN PATROL
THE PENGUIN PATROL! WE'LL REBRAND YOU AS A SOCIETY OF VILLAINS, A TEAM AT THE COMMAND OF YOUR NATURAL LEADER--THE PENGUIN!
IT'S FRESH. IT'S NEW. IT'S A NOW CONCEPT. WHAT DO YOU THINK?
"NATURAL LEADER"?
I WOULDN'T BE CAUGHT DEAD IN THAT SUIT.
THE PENG PATROL!
NOW SEE HERE. THIS WASN'T MY IDEA.

HELLO, DAD? THIS IS BARBARA. CAN YOU SEND SOME MEN DOWN TO THE ABERNATHY BUILDING? WE HAVE SOME UNWELCOME VISITORS AT THE OFFICE.
GOOD WORK, BARBARA. BUT HOW DID YOU SOW DISSENSION IN THEIR RANCOROUS RANKS?
CRIMINALS AREN'T JUST A COWARDLY AND SUPERSTITIOUS LOT, DAD--THEY'RE ILL-EQUIPPED TO DEAL WITH ONE OF THE DEADLIEST FORCES IN EXISTENCE, SOMETHING THAT YOU AND I CAN HANDLE EASILY.
OH? AND WHAT FORCE IS THAT?
OFFIC POLITIC
THE END

YA SEE? IT'S TRUE--THE BOSS, HE'S... HE'S...
FAITH. AND BEGORRAH.
HOLY MORTALITY!
YES, ROBIN. IN OUR LINE OF WORK, IT'S INEVITABLE THAT WE WON'T ALWAYS BE SPARED SUCH A GRUESOME VISAGE.

OUR OLD ENEMY, LOUIE THE LILAC...
...HAS BEEN MURDERED.
"POISON IVY'S DEADLY KISS"
Written by JEFF PARKER Art by JESSE HAMM
Colors by KELLY FITZPATRICK Letters by WES ABBOTT
Cover by MICHAEL and LAURA ALLRED

HOW--HOW DO YOU KNOW IT'S MURDER, CAPED CRUSADER?
IT'S CERTAINLY NOT NATURAL CAUSES, COMMISSIONER. SOME-ONE THE LILAC KNEW... WHO COULD GET IN CLOSE WITHOUT HIM GRABBING A WEAPON.

AND WHO LEFT A VERY DEADLY TRACE.

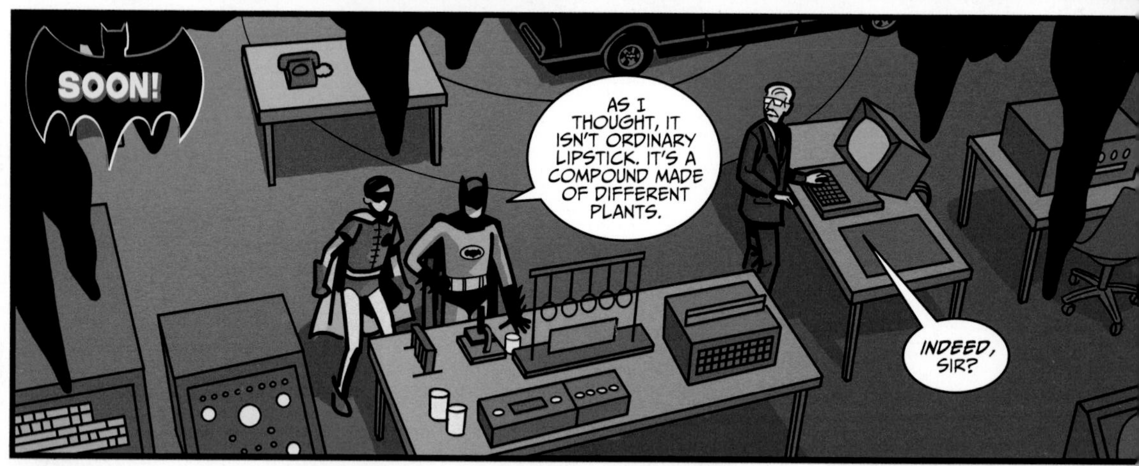
SOON!
AS I THOUGHT, IT ISN'T ORDINARY LIPSTICK. IT'S A COMPOUND MADE OF DIFFERENT PLANTS.
INDEED, SIR?

PARTICULARLY, A FLORAL CHEMICAL FROM ROSA CARULEA. AN EXTREMELY RARE AND DEADLY FLOWERING BUSH.
WHEN ABSORBED BY THE SKIN...
VWEEP
VWEEP
VWEEP

A KISS... FROM A ROSE...
YES, THANK YOU, COMMISSIONER. BATMAN DOES WANT TO BE AT THE QUESTIONING...

R, AT GOTHAM
CE HEADQUARTERS!
"ALL RIGHT, MACURDY, YE WANT TO PLAY HARDBALL, DO YE?"

THERE'S YER WATER... BUT NOT *COLD*, LIKE YE ASKED FOR. ***LUKEWARM.***
I GOT ***RIGHTS,*** O'HARA!

I'LL TAKE OVER QUESTIONING, CHIEF.
GULP!

K, YOU GUYS CAN'T THINK I
ED THE BOSS. I'M THE ONE WHO CALLED IT IN!
NO, WHAT I WANT TO KNOW IS WHERE LOUIE GOT HIS PLANTS.
SEEING YOUR HIDEOUT, THERE WASN'T ENOUGH OF A SETUP TO GROW SUCH SPECIALIZED HYBRIDS.
THE BOSS NEVER TOOK ANY OF US WITH HIM THE NIGHTS HE WENT. HE KEPT HIS SOURCE ***TOP SECRET!***

YOU HAVE TO *THINK!* ANYTHING YOU REMEMBER ABOUT HIS TRIPS.

THERE'S A ***KILLER*** AT LARGE!
I GOT ***NOTHING,*** I MEAN, EXCEPT MAYBE...

"...THAT HE USED TO ALWAYS COME BACK WITH A *CUSTARD*..."
WHAT KIND OF A CLUE IS *THAT?* THERE ARE CUSTARD STANDS ALL OVER GOTHAM. THIS IS *AMERICA!*
THE HENCHMAN MENTIONED LOUIE GOING ON HIS SUPPLY RUNS AT NIGHT, ROBIN. THAT NARROWS IT DOWN TO ONLY ONE BUSINESS.

CUSTARD CAFE
OPEN
ALL-NIGHT
THERE! THAT MUST BE WHERE THE LILAC WOULD STOP FOR HIS SWEET TOOTH.
NOW BEGINS A POSSIBLE LONG NIGHT OF OBSERVATION. SOMEWHERE ALONG THIS ROAD THERE MUST BE AN OPERATION DEVOTED TO HORTICULTURE.
THERE! LOOK!

SHARP EYE, CHUM.
THE OLD *ISLEY NURSERY*... I REMEMBER MY MOTHER COMING OUT HERE FOR THE WAYNE ESTATE GARDENS WHEN I WAS A CHILD.
GOSH.
ISLEY N

-SKELETON
SHOULD WORK
OR THIS...
SO... YOU HAVE BEEN HERE BEFORE?

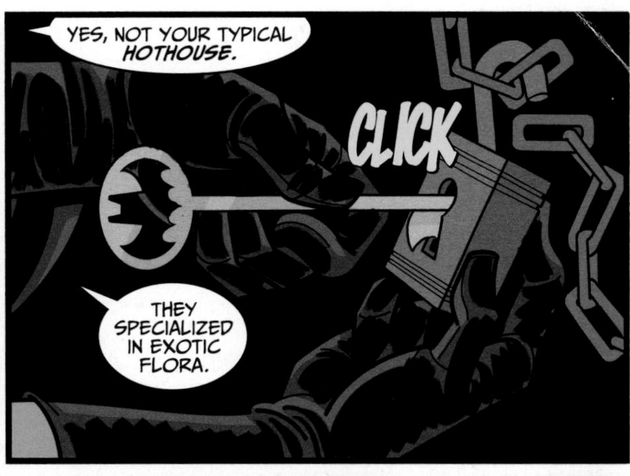
YES, NOT YOUR TYPICAL *HOTHOUSE.*
CLICK
THEY SPECIALIZED IN EXOTIC FLORA.

"THE ISLEYS WERE ESTEEMED BOTANISTS WHO HAD MOVED TO GOTHAM TO TEACH AT THE UNIVERSITY AND START THIS NURSERY."
GREAT, YOU'VE SUCCESSFULLY GRAFTED A STEM, PAMELA!

E'D LOVE TO PLANT ORCHARDS AT WAYNE MANOR.
I'LL COME OUT
O A SOIL STUDY, AND
AN START RIGHT AWAY,
MRS. WAYNE!
"THEY DID VERY WELL FOR MANY YEARS, A FIXTURE OF GOTHAM.

"THEN ONE DAY, DR. ISLEY TOOK ILL...HE HAD BEEN EXPOSED TO THE NETTLES OF A TROPICAL BUSH THAT HAD BEEN MISLABELED AS A HARMLESS PLANT.
"HIS HEALTH NEVER RECOVERED, AND NEITHER DID THE BUSINESS. HIS FAMILY MOVED BACK TO THE SOUTH AND THE NURSERY CLOSED."

WELL, SOMEONE'S SURE USING THE PLACE N--OW!
CAREFUL, BLACKBERRY PLANTS ARE NATURE'S FENCES.

THE GLASS IS ALL FOGGED-UP...
HEAVY CONDENSATION, THE INSIDE MUST BE VERY WARM AND HUMID.

A TROPICAL ENVIRONMENT--THIS COULDN'T BE A RECENT DEVELOPMENT.
SOMEONE WOULD HAVE HAD TO MAINTAIN THESE CONDITIONS OVER THE COURSE OF A YEAR OR MORE...

...THIS MUST BE WHERE LOUI-- URHK!!!
BATMAN!!!

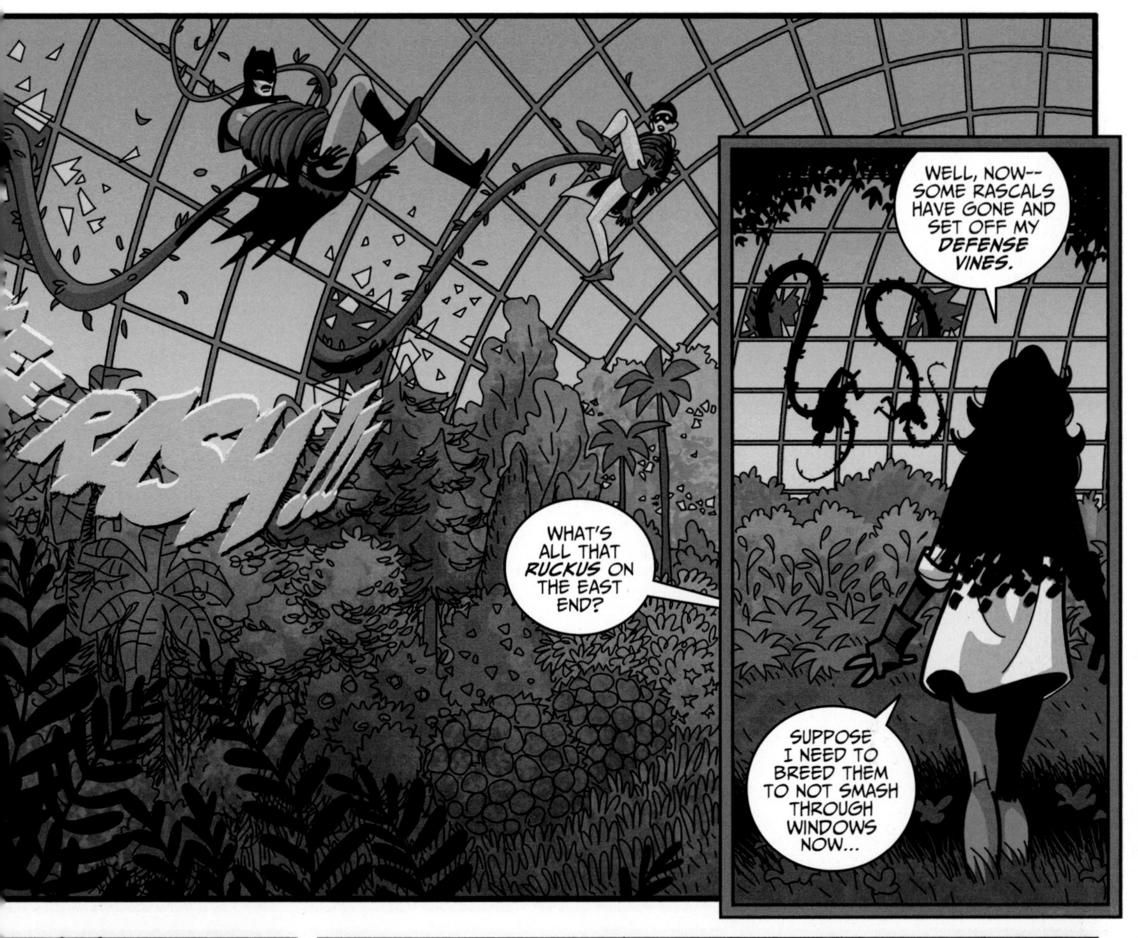

RASH!!!
WHAT'S ALL THAT RUCKUS ON THE EAST END?
WELL, NOW-- SOME RASCALS HAVE GONE AND SET OFF MY DEFENSE VINES.
SUPPOSE I NEED TO BREED THEM TO NOT SMASH THROUGH WINDOWS NOW...
YOU... MUST HAVE BEEN THE ONE SUPPLYING LOUIE THE LILAC WITH HIS FLOWERING WEAPONS!
HE DIDN'T HAVE THE ACUMEN TO GROW SUCH SPECIALIZED FLORA.
THAT WOULD REQUIRE SOMEONE TRAINED FOR YEARS IN THE ADVANCED PRACTICES OF HORTICULTURE...
...POSSIBLY BY HER PARENTS.
YOU'RE RED-HOT, SUGAR BRITCHES.
PAMELA ISLEY.
HOO-WHEE! YOU ARE A GREAT DETECTIVE.
BUT YOU CAN USE MY WORKIN' NAME.

POISON IVY!
I'VE BEEN READYING MY DEBUT IN GOTHAM FOR TWO YEARS NOW, TESTING OUT MY CREATIONS THROUGH THE LILAC...
...WHO RECENTLY THOUGHT HE DIDN'T NEED TO PAY LITTLE OL' IVY FOR HER HARD WORK. SO I LEARNED HIM OTHERWISE.

POISON!
HUSH UP, BOY, I'M TALKIN' TO YOUR BOSS.
'SIDES, I ALREADY SAID IT IN MY NAME. BUT IT AIN'T POISON TO ME.

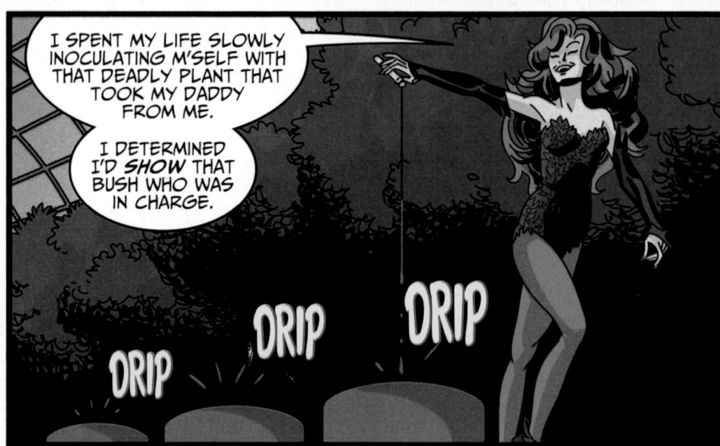
I SPENT MY LIFE SLOWLY INOCULATING M'SELF WITH THAT DEADLY PLANT THAT TOOK MY DADDY FROM ME.
I DETERMINED I'D SHOW THAT BUSH WHO WAS IN CHARGE.
DRIP
DRIP
DRIP

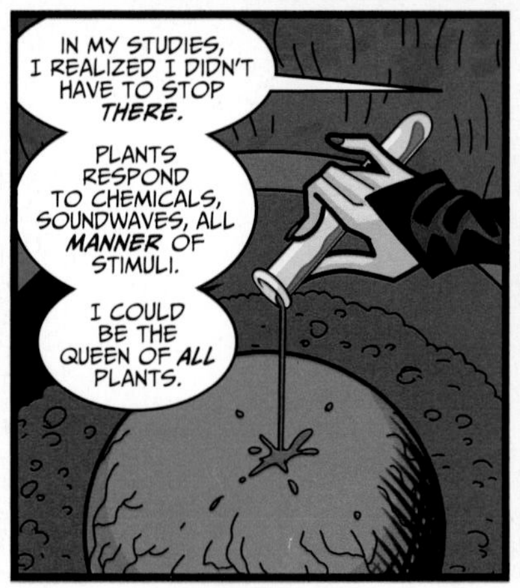
IN MY STUDIES, I REALIZED I DIDN'T HAVE TO STOP THERE.
PLANTS RESPOND TO CHEMICALS, SOUNDWAVES, ALL MANNER OF STIMULI.
I COULD BE THE QUEEN OF ALL PLANTS.

AND I DON'T NEED MIDDLEMEN MAKING ALL THE MONEY WHILE I DO ALL THE REAL WORK.

POP
POP POP!
ALL HAIL POISON IVY!
WE LIVE TO SERVE!
JUST GIVE US WATER AND SUNLIGHT, AND WE'RE READY TO FIGHT!
THIS IS... GHASTLY! GROWING YOUR OWN CRIMINAL FORCE...!
TO WHAT END?
I DIDN'T COME BACK TO GOTHAM FOR OLD TIMES' SAKE, HONEYBUN. I GOT SCORES TO SETTLE.
SPUDS, BRING THOSE BOYS OVER THIS WAY.

THE UNIVERSITY DIDN'T SUPPORT MY DADDY IN HIS TIME OF NEED.
A PITIFUL LI'L SEVERANCE PAY...THEY SHOULDA SCOURED THE GLOBE FOR AN ANTIDOTE.
AFTER ALL HE DID FOR THEM... FOR THIS WHOLE CITY.

VENGEANCE IS A DEAD END, IVY!
BABYDOLL, I KNOW ALL ABOUT DEAD ENDS.
AND AS GOTHAM'S PROTECTOR, YOU'RE ABOUT TO SEE ONE.

I CALL THIS CULTIVATION MY JUPITER FLYTRAP.

MHHRRL
'CAUSE I NEED A WAY BIGGER PLANET THAN VENUS FOR HER NAME!
BYE NOW, YOU HANDSOME HEROES.

EDING TIME FOR THE AMIC DUO?
THE PROBLEM WITH GROWING THE JUPITER FLYTRAP HAS BEEN KEEPING IT *FED!*
YOU TWO HEALTHY RASCALS OUGHT TO FILL IT UP GOOD, THOUGH--IT'LL TAKE...

...HOURS... OH, MY.
THIS ISN'T LIKE THROWING SLABS OF BEEF IN--
--I CAN'T WATCH THIS!

E I'LL GO AHEAD AND START IG OVER GOTHAM NOW THAT HE CITY IS UNPROTECTED.
IYL, YOU AY HERE MAKE SURE Y GET ALL T UP, YA HEAR?
YES, MISS IVY.

BATMAN, IT'S BEEN A REAL TREAT BEING YOUR BEST ENEMY.

BYE, Y'ALL!
OH, NO!

THIS IS IT-- NO ESCAPE!
I'M NEVER GOING TO GROW UP AND INHERIT THE MANTLE OF BATMAN!
AH... EASY, CHUM, LET'S NOT PUT THE CART BEFORE THE HORSE.

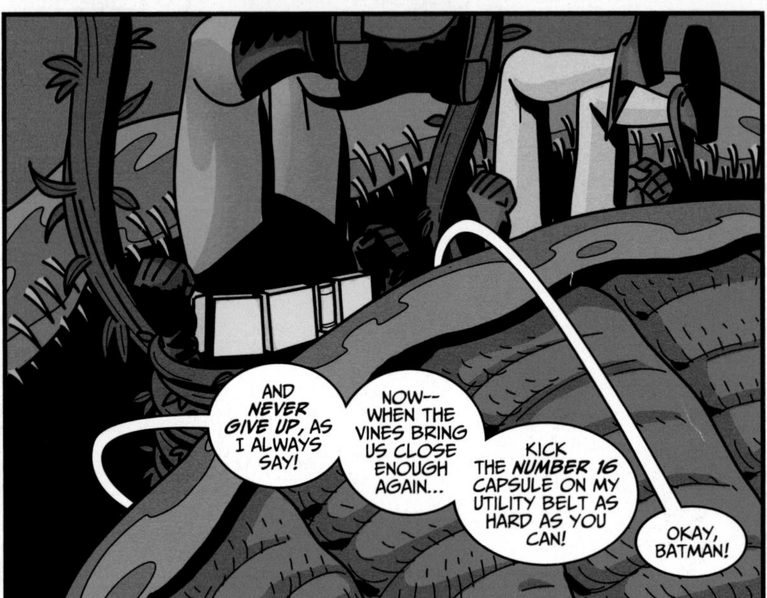
AND NEVER GIVE UP, AS I ALWAYS SAY!
NOW-- WHEN THE VINES BRING US CLOSE ENOUGH AGAIN...
KICK THE NUMBER 16 CAPSULE ON MY UTILITY BELT AS HARD AS YOU CAN!
OKAY, BATMAN!

MOST IMPORTANTLY-- HOLD YOUR BREATH AS SOON AS IT BURSTS!
CLOSER... IF I CAN GET CLOSER...

PSSHHHH
NOW!

WHAT AM THAT?

BATSMAN AND RAWBIN GIVE JUPITER FLYTRAP *GAS!*
IS NOT RIGHT!

BAD PLANT FOOD! NOT GIVE *INJA-JESTION* TO BIG PLANT!

SCHWAM!
NOT... A MOMENT... TOO--

IT *WORKED!* WHAT WAS THAT CAPSULE?
AAAAAWWN...

A CONCENTRATED *HERBICIDE,* ROBIN.
DON'T WASH IT OFF YOUR UNIFORM. I THINK WE'LL NEED IT.
TO THE BATMOBILE!

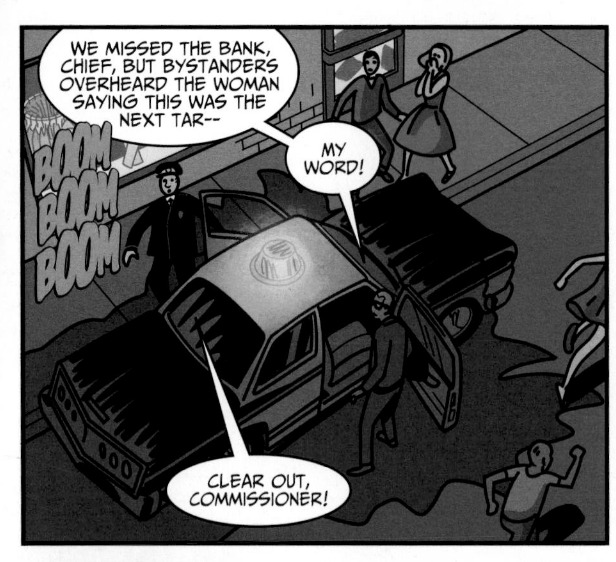
WE MISSED THE BANK, CHIEF, BUT BYSTANDERS OVERHEARD THE WOMAN SAYING THIS WAS THE NEXT TAR--
MY WORD!
CLEAR OUT, COMMISSIONER!
BOOM BOOM BOOM

ME FAVORITE SQUAD CAR!
SORRY, BOYS, Y'ALL CAN'T GO PARKING IN MY PATH, HEAR?
BWOOOOOP!

THESE ROOTS WERE MADE FOR WALKIN'.
NOW GET OUTTA MY WAY OR THESE ROOTS ARE GOING TO WALK ALL OVER YOU, OFFICERS.
BRING THOSE GREENBACKS, MY GREEN BACKS!
AS I LIVE 'N' BREATHE!

OCK du LIEBER
ne clothiers
ASSH!!!
WOO-HOO!

MY FAVORITE KIND OF SALE-- EVERYTHING'S A STEAL.

OH, MY, NOW THIS IS PLUSH!
AND THE BEST PART? NO PLANTS WERE HARMED TO MAKE IT.

THE MEOW WOW WOW
OH, OH! THAT'S CATWOMAN'S OLD NIGHTCLUB!
I HEAR THAT'S THE SWINGINGEST PLACE IN GOTHAM! TIE UP THEM PO-LICE AND LET'S CUT A RUG, FELLAS!
WE GONNA HAVE A MESS OF FUN!

CA-CRUNNCH
AHH!!
LOOK OUT!
EARTHQU

NOW DON'T GO FUSSIN' OR I'LL START CUSSIN'!
POISON IVY LIKES CLIMBING WALLS, Y'ALL.
MY SNORE-SPORES WILL CALM 'EM DOWN-- BUT NOT TOO MUCH, BOYS.
THE NIGHT'S STILL YOUNG.
FFSSHHHH
FFSSH

SAY, THIS PLANT LADY IS FAR OUT!
GEAR!
REMEMBER, KIDS, FLORA EQUALS FUN.

NOW WHICH O YOU FELL IS THE BE DANCER STEP O UP!
DON'T BE PUT O BY MY NAM AIN'T ALW POISON

I THINK LOUIE THE LILAC WOULD BEG TO DIFFER, IVY.
YOU!
Bat-Fact: BAT-NOSTRIL FILTERS KEEP THE SPORES OUT OF BATMAN'S LUNGS!

YOU BETTER NOT HAVE HURT MY LI'L JUPITER FLYTRAP!
WHAM!
OOF!

YOU ARE NOT GOING TO SPOIL MY GOOD TIME! PLANTS-- CRAWL 'EM!
STOP GO-GOING ME, MISS--I HAVE TO HELP BATMAN!

HONEY, THESE AIN'T SOME GLASS-JAW GOONS YOU CAN JUST KNOCK OUT.
MY BOYS WERE GROWN SPECIAL FOR ROUGHHOUSING!
UGH!
WOOMF!

YOU GAVE THEM AN UNNECESSARY WEAKNESS, IVY.

I'M STILL COATED WITH THE HERBICIDE THAT HELPED US ESCAPE YOUR FLYTRAP!
GIVING YOUR HENCHPLANTS MOUTHS AND NOSES ONLY MAKES IT EASIER TO IMPART THE CHEMICAL.
WOOOOHHHH...

HA!
SHOOT! I'M STILL THE MOST BRILLIANT BOTANIST BABE IN BATLAND.

BYE, HONEY PIE!
THANKS FOR THE DANCE!
BOOM BOOM BOOM BOOM

IS THE BATMOBILE IN PLACE?
NO NEED TO ASK WITH OUR FRIEND ON THE JOB, ROBIN.
MAKE THE YOUTH HERE DRINK PLENTY OF WATER TO DILUTE THE EFFECTS OF IVY'S SPORES. I'M GOING AFTER HER.

WELL, T WASN'T D FOR A DEBUT.
GOTHAM IS A LY TOWN. IT'S GOING E SO SWEET BEING IN CHARGE OF IT.
ROMP
OMP
OMP
TROMP

POISON IVY, YOU'RE UNDER ARREST!
HEY!

SORRY, BABY. I'M NOT LEAVING THIS TREE.
I CONGRATULATE YOU, BY THE WAY--DEVELOPING A COSTA RICAN WALKING TREE THAT ACTUALLY WALKS...IMPRESSIVE.

BUT WE'RE KING TO POLICE EADQUARTERS.
NO, TURN RIGHT, DANG IT! WHY'S MY TREE GOING THIS WAY?
VRRRM
VROOM!!!

YOUR TREE STILL CRAVES SUNLIGHT--
--EVEN THE KIND EMITTED BY THE GROW-LAMP MOUNTED ON MY BATMOBILE!
VERY GOOD, SIR.

WHEE! YOU ARE A SWINGER!
WELL, THE FUN IS OVER, POISON IVY!
WE TAKE A DIM VIEW OF MURDER IN GOTHAM CITY.

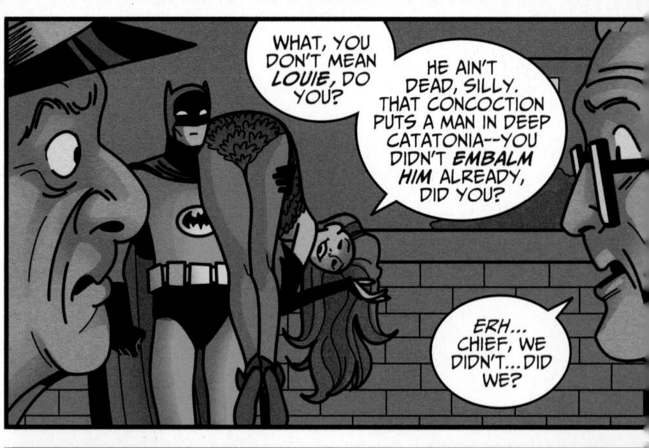
WHAT, YOU DON'T MEAN LOUIE, DO YOU?
HE AIN'T DEAD, SILLY. THAT CONCOCTION PUTS A MAN IN DEEP CATATONIA--YOU DIDN'T EMBALM HIM ALREADY, DID YOU?
ERH... CHIEF, WE DIDN'T... DID WE?

SOON!
SEE, THE MOSS REVERSES THE EFFECT!
WUH... WHERE AM I...
LILAC

INCREDIBLE. YOUR FORMIDABLE SKILL COULD BE A BOON TO SCIENCE INSTEAD OF CRIME.
AW, WHERE'S THE FUN IN THAT? SO NOW YOU KNOW IT AIN'T FATAL...

GOSH!
ALL RIGHT, THIS AIN'T A PARTY, LET'S GO!

ALL
RED

ACROSS THE BORDER LIVES A LEGEND...
...A MAN WITH THE POWER OF TEN, A MAN WHO CASTS A SHADOW OF FEAR.
AS FAR AS GOTHAM CITY, THE WIND CARRIES HIS NAME...
BANE!
BANE?
BANE.
SOUTH AMERI
BOL
PARAGUAY
URUGUAY
BASIN

NOW, BATMAN MUST FACE HIS GREATEST CHALLENGE!
YOU...TRICKED ME...WOULDN'T HAVE SHOWN YOU...THE CRYSTAL SKULL...IF I'D HEARD YOUR... LAUGH...

HA HA-- HEY!

SAY!
RIP!
WHSHHH
YOUR CUNNING KNOWS NO BOUNDS...

...RIDDLER!
THE DOGMATIC DUO, BACK TO BADGER ME YET AGAIN!
I WAS GOING TO PAY FOR THIS SKULL, I'LL HAVE YOU KNOW!

WAK!
A LIKELY STORY-- YOW!
I'LL GIVE YOU THAT, ROBIN-- I WASN'T GOING TO GIVE THE ASKING PRICE OF FIVE THOUSAND DOLLARS.

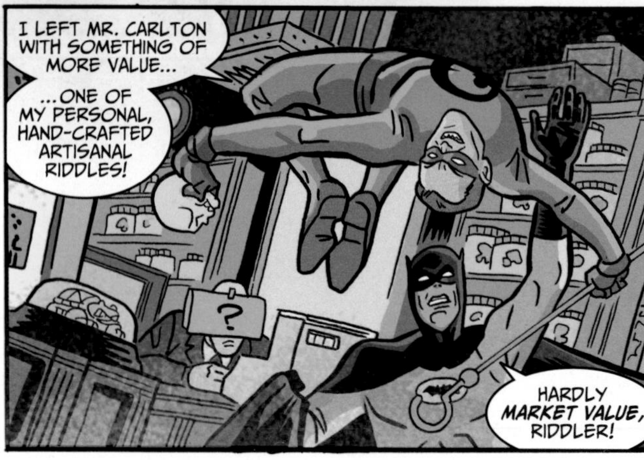
I LEFT MR. CARLTON WITH SOMETHING OF MORE VALUE...
...ONE OF MY PERSONAL, HAND-CRAFTED ARTISANAL RIDDLES!
HARDLY MARKET VALUE, RIDDLER!

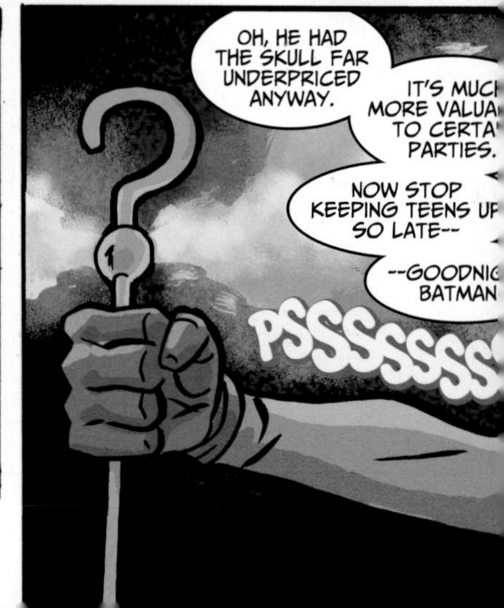
OH, HE HAD THE SKULL FAR UNDERPRICED ANYWAY.
IT'S MUCH MORE VALUA TO CERTA PARTIES.
NOW STOP KEEPING TEENS UP SO LATE--
--GOODNIG BATMAN
PSSSSSSS

NEW DAY!
MY HEAD IS STILL POUNDING FROM RIDDLER'S GAS!
DRINK MORE WATER, CHUM.

WE NEED CLEAR MINDS TO PARSE THIS LATEST RIDDLE.
"FRIDAY-- STEALING SKULLS IS NO SMALL THING--NOW TO WATCH A MAN... STEAL A RING!"
STUFF AND NONSENSE, TRYIN' TO LEAD US ASTRAY.

NEVER *NONSENSE,* CHIEF O'HARA. THE RIDDLER HAS A MENTAL BLOCK THAT COMPELS HIM TO ADMIT HIS FIENDISH GOALS.
FRIDAY
STEALING SKULLS IS NO SMALL THING-- NOW TO WATCH A MAN... STEAL A RING!
The Riddler
BUT HIS PUZZLE-OBSESSED MIND CONTORTS THOSE TRUTHS INTO RIDDLES IN AN ATTEMPT TO STAY SECRET.

...FRIDAY! SO WHATEVER HE'S PLANNING HAPPENS *TONIGHT.*
TO STEAL A RING... MAYBE HE'S GOING TO HIT *POURTIN'S JEWELERS?*
MAYBE IT'S NOT THAT KIND OF *RING,* BOY WONDER.

MIND IF I JOIN IN? I MAY HAVE SOME INTRIGUING DETAILS.
BATGIRL!
AS I LIVE AND BREATHE!

THANK YOU, BATMAN.
MY PLEASURE, BATGIRL.
I'M ALWAYS INTERESTED IN WHAT YOUR KEEN EAR FOR CRIMEFIGHTING HAS HEARD.

THERE'S BEEN A LOT OF BUZZ ON THE STREETS ABOUT WHAT RIDDLER'S UP TO.

MOSTLY FROM HENCHME
ANGRY HE DIDN'T HIRE THE
COMMISSIONER, I BELIEV
YOU HAVE A NEWSPAPER
IN YOUR TOP RIGHT
DRAWER?
WH-WHY
YES, HO
DID YOU
KNOW?

I READ THE NEWS, THERE WAS NOTHING BIG HAPPENING...
NOT THE MAIN NEWS, ROBIN-- *THIS.*
LOCAL SPORTS AND ENTERTAINMENT.

A *WRESTLING RING!*
RIGHT. TONIGHT'S TITLE CARD MATCH FEATURES THE CURRENT BELT-HOLDING CHAMPION, *THE HANGMAN,* VERSUS A NEW CONTENDER...
The Gotham Times
HANGMAN FACES HEAVY MYSTERY MAN FROM MEXICO

...CALLED *BANE.*

FRIDAY NIGHT!
JUST IN TIME, THE MATCH IS ABOUT TO START!
HOW DID WE GET SUCH GREAT SEATS?
HOLY COW, BATMAN! I NEVER HAD YOU PEGGED FOR A WRASSLIN' FAN!
GRAPPLING HAS BEEN AN HONORED CHALLENGE SINCE THE GRECO-ROMAN OLYMPICS, CITIZEN.
AAANNND THE RETURNIN' CHAMPEEN, THE GOTHAM GRINDER...
...THE HAAAANGMAAAAN!
ROUND 1
WOOO!!
HISSSS!
HANG-MAN!
AND NOW, FOR THE FIRST TIME IN THIS VENUE, MAYBE THIS COUNTRY, THE BRUISER FROM BELOW THE BORDER...

BAAANNE!
GASP!
LOOK HOW BIG HE IS!
HE CAN'T TAKE THE HANGMAN, FORGET IT!
"HE'S A LUCHADORE-- THIS COULD BE SERIOUS!"
POP CORN
"BANE ENTERS THE RING"
Written by JEFF PARKER
Art and Color by SCOTT KOWALCHUK
Letters by WES ABBOTT
Cover by MICHAEL and LAURA ALLRED

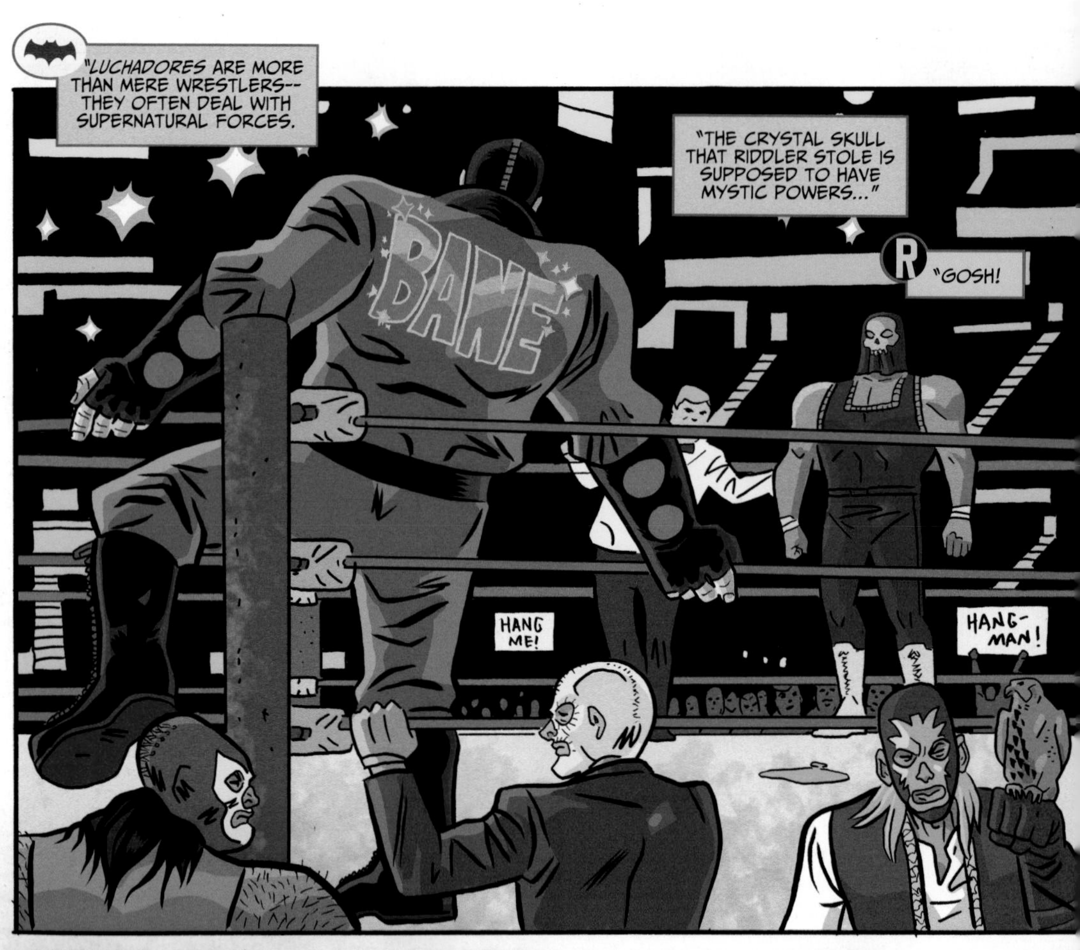
"LUCHADORES ARE MORE THAN MERE WRESTLERS-- THEY OFTEN DEAL WITH SUPERNATURAL FORCES.
"THE CRYSTAL SKULL THAT RIDDLER STOLE IS SUPPOSED TO HAVE MYSTIC POWERS..."
"GOSH!
BANE
HANG ME!
HANG-MAN!

AND LOOK WHO'S BANE'S CORNER MAN!

HEEHEHEHEHEEE! THE HANGMAN IS A 12-1 FAVORITE, I'M GOING TO CLEAN UP ON THIS FIGHT!
JUST MAKE SURE EL CRANEO ES SAFE, RIDDLER.

DING DING DING DING!
GENTLEMEN... BEGIN!
WHOOOM!

SHOULDN'T WE GO ARREST RIDDLER?
HE'S STAYING PUT, NO NEED TO RILE THE CROWD--LET'S WAIT UNTIL THE MATCH IS FINISHED.

DING! DING!

I THINK YOU MIGHT WANT TO REFRESH BEFORE THIS ROUND!
POP!
ALREADY? EHH, I WAS GOING TO BEAT HIM ANYWAY.

SLLRRRRP
AHH.

GOT--
YOU!
SAY GOODBYE TO OXYGEN, CHUMP! YOU'RE IN THE HANGMAN'S NOOSE!
WRNNCH

HA HAHAH HAAAA!

AAAAAHHHH
WAM!
HOOHOO HOOHOO HAHA!
"HOLY HURLING HANGMAN!"
DING DING
DING DING DING

BATMAN, TOO?
WOW!
I'M NOT SURE IF THAT COUNTS UNDER THE MALLEABLE RULES OF WRESTLING...
NOLAN
...BUT I DON'T THINK HANGMAN IS RETURNING, SO I'M TAKING THIS BREAK TO ARREST THE RIDDLER.

DON'T LET HIM TAKE ME--YOU NEED ME!
SI.

I UNDERSTAND THIS IS YOUR FIRST TIME IN GOTHAM, BANE...
...BUT HARBORING A FUGITIVE IS A CRIME HERE.

WE LEAVE SOON, BATMAN. ALL YOU HAVE TO DO...

...IS GET OUT OF THE WAY, EY?
CLOTHES
LINE!

BATMAN!
GASP!

HA! YOU'RE NOT UP AGAINST UNDERPAID GOONS THIS TIME, BATTY!
YOU'RE FACING THE MIGHT OF A PRO WRESTLER!

NO, MAKE IT STOP!
BATMAN, HE'S A PRO WRESTLER!
WAM
BAM
CAN'T SOMEONE DO SOMETHING?
KOOJJ!!
YOU FIGHT WELL, BAT, BUT I AM THE GREATEST PRO--
¿--QUE ES ESTO?
FWHIP
FWHIP
WE'VE GOT HIM!
HEH HEH HEH.
BATGIRL! ROBIN! NO!!

K.O.'d
WA-BOOOM!
K.O.'d
¡VAMOS!
WOOOSH!
WOOOSH!
DIS
HEEEEEEE HEHEHEHEHEHE HEEEEE!!!
YOU WERE THE GREATEST CHAMPION, BATMAN... BUT NO MORE.
NOW THE WORLD WILL FEAR THE NAME OF
BANE!
CAN THIS BE HAPPENING? BATMAN BEATEN BY A BRAWLING BRUTE!?!
BREAK HIM!
DOES THE RULE OF LAW EVEN APPLY ANYMORE?

EEP IN THE MYSTERIOUS YUCATAN OF MEXICO, IN EL CIUDAD DEL CRANEO...
BANE RETURNS! DID YOU HEAR?
"THE BATMAN, HE JUMPED INTO THE RING WITH BANE...
EL CRACK!
"...AND WAS BROKEN IN TWO!!!
BANE IS THE CHAMPION OF THE ENTIRE WESTERN HEMISPHERE!
WE WILL NEVER BE FREE.
I, AH, HOPE I CAN STAY AWHILE, SEÑOR BANE.
AIDING YOU IN HOSPITALIZING BATMAN FOR LIFE MAKES THE STATES A LITTLE TOO HOT FOR ME, NOW.
YOU MAY LIVE LIKE A KING HERE, RIDDLER.
AND I... LIKE A MIGHTY SUPER-KING!
NONE WILL CHALLENGE ME...

"...NOW THAT I HAVE DESTROYED THE BATMAN!"
WOW! YOU'RE RIGHT, BATMAN-- BY HAVING THE BAT BOAT SENT DOWN HERE, WE CAN COVER A LOT MORE TERRITORY QUICKLY!
TRANSPORT TOOK A LOT OF TIME, BUT COMMISSIONER GORDON AND CHIEF O'HARA ARE DOWN HERE BY NOW, ALREADY ON BANE'S TRAIL.
BANE HAS BEEN EASY TO TRACK NOW THAT HE FEELS UNBEATABLE, BATGIRL.
THIS HAS ALSO GIVEN ME TIME TO RESEARCH AND FIND SOME INTERESTING HISTORY ON THE OBJECT HE BROUGHT BACK.
I HAVE TO ADMIT, BATMAN, IT WAS PRETTY SCARY WHEN WE THOUGHT YOU WERE FINISHED!
I IMAGINE SO, OLD CHUM.
I'VE ALWAYS KEPT MY BATARANG HANDILY TUCKED IN THE BACK OF MY UTILITY BELT...
...LITTLE DID I KNOW ONE DAY THAT PRACTICE WOULD SAVE MY SPINE
I'LL TRY AGAIN TO RAISE O'HARA AND GORDON ON THE BAT-RADIO...
...BY NOW, THEY MAY HAVE INFILTRATED BANE'S HOME VILLAGE.

THAT MOMENT,
SKULL CITY...
IT'S WORKING, CHIEF-- THE LOCALS ARE ALREADY ACCEPTING US AS THEIR OWN.
SURE, AND WE'LL FIND THAT LECHEROUS LUCHADOR NOW!
DO NOT LAUGH, BETO. THEY MAY HAVE HEAD INJURIES.
IMOENCH.

OLÉ, ME AMIGOS, HAVE NY OF YE SEEN THIS BANE LAD--
NO, NO! SILENCIO, SEÑOR!

RAMON, HABLAS INGLES.
SIRS, DON'T ASK AROUND ABOUT BANE. HE AND HIS MEN ARE BAD NEWS.
THEY HAVE JUST RETURNED FROM YOUR COUNTRY.

BANE!
BANE!
BANE!
AND THERE THEY ARE.
THE RIDDLER IS WITH HIM!
LOOK! THE BANEMOBILE!

BEHOLD!
I HAVE RETURNED THE OTHER CRYSTAL SKULL TO ITS HOME!

COME IN, COMMISSIONER, COME IN, COMMISSIONER GORDON-- FSSZK--

EH?

HOOHOO HOO HOOOOO!!! LOOK--WHO--HAS... A PASSPORT!
COMMISSIONER GORDON, YOU'RE FAR OUTSIDE YOUR JURISDICTION!
WAK
ER, UM--

YOU SHOULD HAVE STAYED IN GOTHAM, POLICÍA.
LOCK THEM IN THE PYRAMID WITH THE OTHERS.
TOO BAD FOR YOU, GRINGOS.

YOU WILL NEVER LEAV THE SKULL CITY!
GASP --DAD!

TONIGHT, WE SHOW OUR RESPECT TO THE MIGHTY HERO-KING OF SKULL CITY...
...THE UNSTOPPABLE BANE!

BUT BEFORE THE MAIN EVENT, WE HAVE BOUTS WITH LESSER *LUCHADORES*. FIRST UP, ***MIL MASCARAS*** VS. ***EL SANTO***...

THEY MAY HAVE LOST THE BAT-RADIO, BUT THE TRACER YOU PUT ON CHIEF O'HARA SAYS THEY'RE IN HERE.
AND TO THINK, I FELT BAD SNEAKING THAT TRACER ONTO HIM YESTERDAY.
DON'T, ROBIN.
GOOD POLICE ARE TOO VALUABLE TO LOSE.

I HEAR VOICES DOWN *THAT* WAY.

HERE!
YE *FOUND* US! SAINTS BE *PRAISED!*
YOU SEE, MAYOR MARTINE? THE BATMAN NEVER FAILS!
BIENVENIDOS, CAPED CRUSADERS!

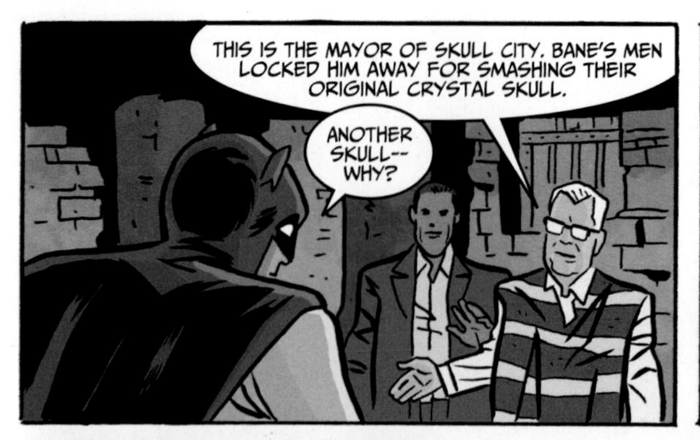
THIS IS THE MAYOR OF SKULL CITY. BANE'S MEN LOCKED HIM AWAY FOR SMASHING THEIR ORIGINAL CRYSTAL SKULL.
ANOTHER SKULL-- WHY?

THE CRYSTAL SKULL IS THE SECRET TO MAKING THE ELIXIR WHICH GIVES BANE HIS GREAT POWER!
IT LASTS ONLY A FEW MINUTES AFTER DRINKING, BUT DURING THAT TIME, BANE IS UNBEATABLE. IT IS HOW HE HAS DOMINATED THE WRESTLING CIRCUIT HERE...

"...AND MY CITY."
VENOM
ALBERT DESMOND

THAT SOUNDS LIKE THE EXACT ANCIENT PRACTICE I READ OF, WHERE AZTEC PRIESTS SENT MIGHTY WARRIORS INTO BATTLE.
I PREPARED FOR THAT THIS TIME--
BANE! BANE! BANE!

HOORRAAAYYY
ÁNDALE...
BANE
"BANE IS TAKING THE STAGE--HE WILL EASILY DEFEAT YET ANOTHER CHALLENGER WHO WANTS TO SET MY CITY FREE."

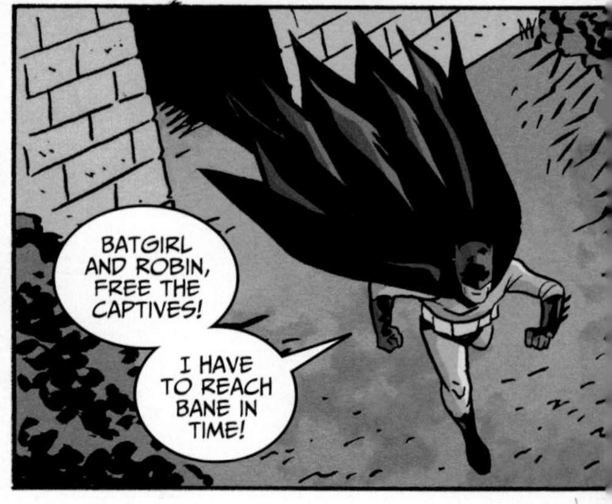
BATGIRL AND ROBIN, FREE THE CAPTIVES!
I HAVE TO REACH BANE IN TIME!

TONIGHT, BANE WILL PROVE HIS GREAT MIGHT ONCE AND FOR ALL!
HE WILL TAKE ON ALL OTHER LUCHADORES WHO DARE CHALLENGE HIM!
HEE HEE HEH, IT'S JUICE TIME!

OLD, MIS MIGOS!
LET ME TAKE THE FIRST ROUND!
BATMAN!

HOW IS THIS?! I BROKE YOUR BACK!
QUICK, BIG GUY, TAKE A SLUG!

YOU BROKE MY BEST BATARANG, BANE.
BUT THAT FREED UP UTILITY BELT SPACE FOR ANOTHER DEVICE I'VE DESIGNED.
WHOOOSH!

CLACK-CLACK-CLACK

MMMGHH!

UN-FAIR!!!

FWAP!
VERY FAIR, RIDDLER!
FWAP!
NOW, THERE IS NO CRYSTAL SKULL SERUM, JUST OUR KNOWLEDGE OF MARTIAL COMBAT.
WHOOM!

WHOMF!
GOOD THIN BANE IS STIL INCREDIBL STRONG, THEN, HEH HEEE!!

AND I'M--USING THAT--
--TO GET INTO--
WANNNG!

--POSITION!
KER-WHAM!
BAT-MAN!
HA-HA!
AT-MAN!
GASP!
GO, BATMAN!
WRNCH!
T-MAN!
WRAK
WAM
BAT-MAN!

CLACK

NO!
I HAVE A FLIGHT TO CATCH!
SORRY, RIDDLER.
WE'RE COMING TO HELP, BATMAN!

NO, ROBIN. THIS IS NOT TRULY OUR FIGHT.
TIME TO TURN IT OVER TO THOSE WHO HAVE WAITED FOR AN *EVEN FIELD* TO DEFEND THEIR HOME!
MIL GRACIAS, BATMAN!

HA HAA! FREEDOM!!
BAH.
WOW, THEY'RE REALLY LETTING BANE *HAVE* IT!
YES, THIS IS THE TRUE MEANING OF *LUCHA LIBRE*... FREE WRESTLING!

BRR-
LONNNG

O HAS THE AUDACITY TO ROB... POLICE HEADQUARTERS?!?
WE GOT YOUR CALL, COMMISSIONER! WHO'S THE THIEF?
HE TOOK TH' CONFISCATED BANK BAGS, NOTHIN' WE CAN DO!
IT'S THE END TIMES, CHIEF!
OVER THERE--GOSH! RIGHT IN FRONT OF THE WHOLE POLICE DEPARTMENT!
YOU THERE--STOP AND SURRENDER!
HEH, HEH.
I INVITED THE OFFICERS TO STOP ME, BUT THEY WERE ALL TOO AFRAID, BATMAN.
GOOD TO FINALLY MEET YOU. I AM THE SCARECROW.
"SCARECROW COMES TO TOWN"
Written by JEFF PARKER Art by LUKAS KETNER
Colors by KELLY FITZPATRICK
Letters by WES ABBOTT
Cover by MICHAEL and LAURA ALLRED

HOW...HE WAS RIGHT HERE, I HAD HIM...
YOU FAILED! YOU FAILED ME AND ALL OF GOTHAM CITY!
OUR VILLAINS ARE RIGHT--YOU ARE THE BOY BLUNDER.
THAT'S IT, NO MORE SIDEKICK WASTING MY TIME! YOU'RE OFF THE TEAM!
NO MORE ROBIN!!!!
ROBIN
ROBIN
ROBIN
NOOOOOOOOOO
STARRING
ADAM WEST
THAT WAS A GOOD SHOW, WASN'T IT?
OUR BOY SURE LIKED IT.
YES, BUT-- NO! MOM, DAD! DON'T GO THIS WAY!
PLEASE, PLEASE, TURN BACK!
BUT, SON THE CAR IS WAY...
NOOOOOOOOOO

--SO... REAL! BUT-- IT WAS THE GAS.
ROBIN, HEAR MY VOICE, SHAKE IT OFF!
BATMAN AN' ROBIN HAVE LEFT GOTHAM!
THE CITY IS DOOMED, WILL NO ONE PROTECT US?!
THE FIEND! HE MEANS TO EXPOSE ALL OF GOTHAM TO HIS FEAR GAS.
IN 3 DAYS THE WHOLE CITY WILL FEAR THE SCARECROW!
COME, ROBIN, I'LL EXAMINE THE TRACE CHEMICALS OUR CLOTHES NO DOUBT ABSORBED.
TO THE BATMOBILE!
ON, AT THE CRET CRIME AB OF THE ATCAVE...
SUCH... A STRANGE... COMPOUND.
WEARING FILTERS WOULD BE USELESS, THE TOXIN CAN AFFECT ONE EASILY THROUGH THE SKIN.
THE BAT-COMPUTER HAS FOUND THE MOST LIKELY SOURCE OF THE RAW MATERIALS YOU ENTERED.
DING!
A SMALL TOWN IN THE APPALACHIAN MOUNTAINS.
CHARGE THE ATOMIC BATTERIES, ROBIN... WE'RE TAKING A ROAD TRIP.

A BEAUTIFUL DRIVE ACROSS AMERICA'S SCENIC BYWAYS!
WELCOME TO GOTHAM CITY
JITTERS HOLLER
YOU'UNS AIN'T FROM AROUND CHERE, ARE YA?
WE'RE CRIMEFIGHTERS FROM GOTHAM CITY, SIR.
THE SOIL HERE HAS UNUSUAL PROPERTIES THAT WE THINK ARE BEING USED AGAINST INNOCENTS IN OUR HOME.
EUSTACE, THAT'S THE BAT-MAN! YOU INVITE HIM IN FOR SOME SUPPER.
I WAS A GONNA, MAW!
WE WOULD BE OBLIGED.
THIS IS DELICIOUS... BUT WHAT ARE GRITS?
HOMINY, SON!
GROUND CORNMEAL, ROBIN. A FINE COUNTERPART TO THIS SWEET ICED TEA.
NOW, YOU SAY YOU'VE HAD PROBLEMS WITH CROPS GROWN HERE AFFECTING OUTSIDERS BEFOR MR. COBBLETOE?
OH, THEY ALWAYS FUSS, SAYI OUR PRODUCE GIVE 'EM THE JITTERS.

SEE, ALL THE CROPS AROUND HERE--CORN, MOSTLY--IS IRRIGATED BY A MINERAL SPRING THAT WE ALL USE.
IT STARTS OVER YONDER, BY THE OLD *CRANE* LAND.
IS ANYONE LIVING THERE NOW?

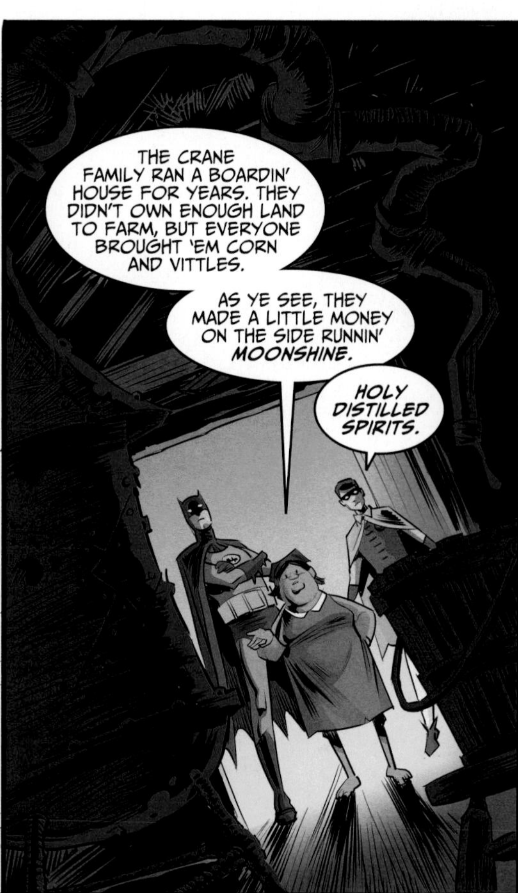
THE CRANE FAMILY RAN A BOARDIN' HOUSE FOR YEARS. THEY DIDN'T OWN ENOUGH LAND TO FARM, BUT EVERYONE BROUGHT 'EM CORN AND VITTLES.
AS YE SEE, THEY MADE A LITTLE MONEY ON THE SIDE RUNNIN' ***MOONSHINE.***
HOLY DISTILLED SPIRITS.

"ONE A' THEIR BOARDERS RAN OUT IN THE MIDDLE O' THE NIGHT--AND LEFT THEIR BABYCHILD IN A *TATER SACK!*
"MISS CRANE TOOK CARE OF IT BEST SHE COULD, BUT SHE HAD SO MUCH WORK TO DO, LITTLE JONNY WAS ON HIS OWN MOST THE TIME.
TAIK GOOD CARE A HIM

"HER ROTTEN BOY PICKED ON HIM, KEPT THE POOR YOUNG'UN ***AFEARED,*** DAY AND NIGHT."
WHY YA *RUNNIN',* LI'L JON? WHAT'S YER *HURRY?*
HAW HAW!

"BUT HE WAS A BRIGHT 'UN. LATER, HE GOT HIMSELF A SCHOLARSHIP AND WENT OFF YOUR WAY TO SCHOOL."

"I THOUGHT WE'D SEEN THE LAST O' JON, BUT HE TURNED UP A COUPLE O' MONTHS AGO--COLLECTED SOMETHIN' FROM THE SHED. THE PECULIAR THING WAS RIGHT AFTER HE LEFT...

"ZEKE CRANE CAME UP HERE JUST A-WAILIN'."
BIG OL' SPIDERS, EVERYWHERE! GET 'EM OFF ME!
"HE HAD TO BE PUT UNDER WATCH DOWN AT THE HOSPITAL FOR NERVES 'N' HEAD AILMENTS."

LISTEN TO ME, JUST A-GOSSIPIN'! SORRY, DE-TECTIVES.
THANKS FOR YOUR HELP, MAW. WE BETTER BE GOING, TO MAKE IT BACK TO GOTHAM IN TIME.
NOT SO FAST, ROBIN. I HAVE A LITTLE MORE INVESTIGATING TO DO...
...AND I WOULD LOVE TO HAVE SECOND HELPINGS OF YOUR GRITS.
WHY, SHORE!
?
HURRY, BATMAN! FOR THE NEXT EVENING IN GOTHAM CITY...

WHY DO YOU RUN, GOTHAM?
WHAT IS YOUR HURRY?!
DO YOU NO LONGER FEEL SAFE IN YOUR HOME?
NOW YOU KNOW THE TRUE NATURE OF THE WORLD, THE WAY I SEE IT.
GHOSTS, I SEE GHOSTS EVERYWHERE!
WAH-HAAA!!
!
MAKE IT STOP!
BEES, BEES, BEES!
LUV BUGGY
YOU ALL ARCH AROUND IKE KINGS OF E EARTH, AS IF EVERYTHING IS FINE.
THAT IS NOT THE TRUE NATURE OF THE WORLD. I BUT HAVE TO PEEL BACK YOUR VENEER OF CALM AND COMPOSURE TO SEE WHAT LIES UNDER.
WHAT'S THERE IS WHAT DRIVES EVERY CHOICE YOU MAKE.
YOUR FEAR.

EH? WHY IS MY FEAR GAS FIZZLING?
FFSSSSST

I HAVE ENOUGH TANKS OF FEAR FLUID IN THE SEWER TO KEEP THE CITY IN TERROR FOR WEEKS!
DID RATS CHEW THE LINES?

NO... NOT RATS, JONATHAN.
SEWER
WH-WHAT--
WHY DO YOU USE THAT... NAME!

YOU ARE NOT THE SCARECROW, JONATHAN CRANE...
...I AM!

YOU RIED TO OME THE NG THAT FEAR, BUT AREN'T ME!
NO... **NO!** YOU WERE NEVER REAL! IT WAS JUST ZEKE...

I JUST DO WHAT TH' SCARECROW **TELLS** ME, JONNY! I CARRY HIM 'ROUND...
...LIKE WHEN HE'D TELL ME TO SET HIM OUTSIDE YER WINDOW...
NO, **NO, NOO--**

AAAAAAAAAAA

HHHHHHNNNNHH...
GOSH!

BRINGING BACK HIS MEMORIES SHUT HIM DOWN, LIKE YOU SAID, BATMAN!
I DID NOT RELISH DOING THAT, BUT HE WAS TAKING OUT HIS ISSUES ON OUR FAIR CITY.
HE USED THE DISTILLED CORN FROM JITTERS HOLLOW, REFINED TO MAXIMUM POTENCY.
EATING THE GRITS HELPED INURE US TO THE FEAR GAS, ENOUGH TO EMPLOY MENTAL EXERCISES AND RESIST IT.
THE KIND OF DEFENSES IT TOOK CRANE A LIFETIME TO ADOPT.

SOON, AT ARKHAM INSTITUTE...
HAD CRANE BEEN RELATED TO THE CITIZENS OF THE VALLEY, HE WOULD SURELY HAVE HAD THE NATURAL RESISTANCE TO THE MODIFIED STARCH...
...AND AVOIDED HIS YOUTHFUL TRAUMA. CLASSIC RECIPROCATION, SUBJECTING THE WORLD TO HIS OWN PAST.
ANOTHER BRILLIANT MIND WASTED, THAT COULD BE USED TO HELP SOCIETY. DO YOUR BEST, DR. HUGO.
NOT.

NOT...
...AFRAID.
THE END

ROUTINE MONEY
ANSFER BECOMES
METHING UNUSUAL!
GET BACK!
MIKE? WHAT'S GOING ON OUT THERE?

DON'T OPEN THE RUCK, IKE, HE'S--
AAGHH!!
MIKE! WHAT'S HAPPENING?!

KRUNCH!!
WHO'S THAT? DON'T COME IN, OR I'LL FIRE!
I MEAN IT!!

BLAM!
BACK! *BACK!!!*
BLAM!
BLAM!

EEYYAAHH!!!

BEEP
BEEP
BEEP

BEEN A WHILE SINCE WE USED THE BAT-SIGNAL.
HEAVEN HELP US IF IT DOESN'T WORK, CHIEF.

I'M SORRY, COMMISSIONER. THE BATMAN IS ON PATROL IN TOWN TONIGHT.
THANK YOU, MYSTERY ATTENDANT. I'LL TRY OTHER MEANS.

PLEASE LOOK TO THE SKIES, MASKED MANHUNTER!

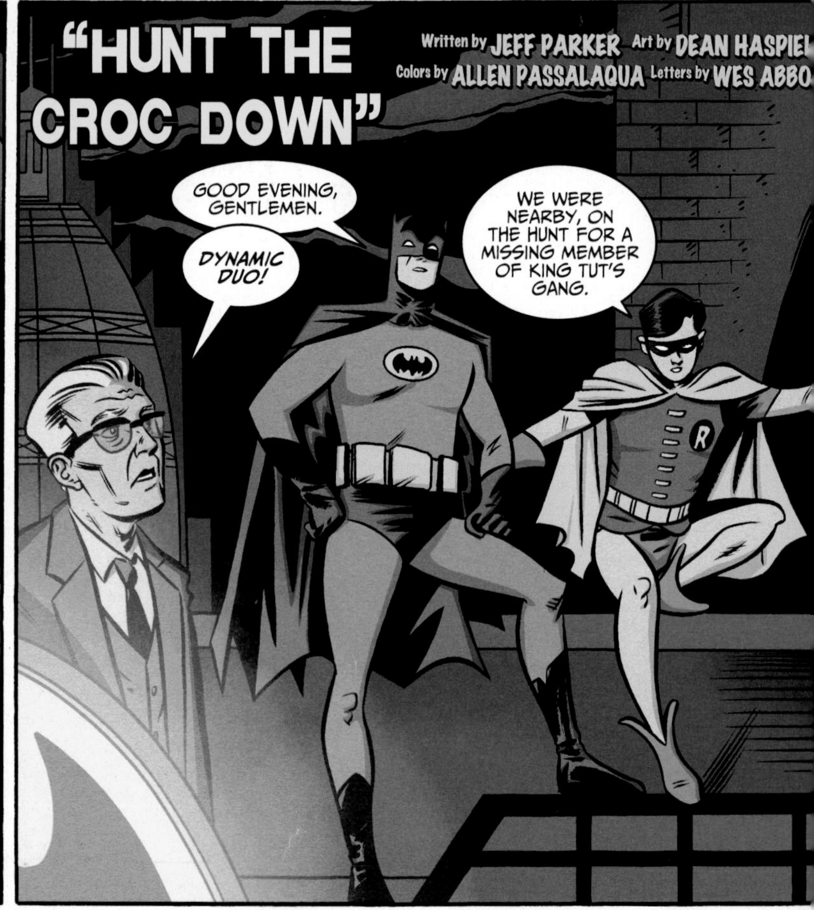
"HUNT THE CROC DOWN"
Written by JEFF PARKER Art by DEAN HASPIEL
Colors by ALLEN PASSALAQUA Letters by WES ABBO
GOOD EVENING, GENTLEMEN.
DYNAMIC DUO!
WE WERE NEARBY, ON THE HUNT FOR A MISSING MEMBER OF KING TUT'S GANG.

I BELIEVE AN EVEN MORE SERIOUS THREAT IS AT LARGE, BOY WONDER.
REPORTS OF A *MONSTER-MAN* ON A *RAMPAGE!*
SOME SAY IT'S A *LIVIN' DINOSAUR!*

THAT'S WHAT THE GUARDS DESCRIBED AT THE ARMORED CAR ROBBERY. IMAGINE!
WHAT WOULD A *DINOSAUR* WANT WITH *MONEY?*

ELIEVE WE ALREADY ON THIS EATURE'S TRAIL.
ONE OF TUT'S HENCHMEN DRANK AN ANCIENT EGYPTIAN ELIXIR THAT HORRIBLY TRANSFORMED HIM.
COME, ROBIN. THERE IS ONE MORE PLACE I WANTED TO INVESTIGATE.

ATER, AT THE THER END OF TOWN...
WHOSE HOME IS THIS?
A *LADY-FRIEND* OF THE MAN WE WERE ALREADY PURSUING.

WELL, I DIDN'T EXPECT *BATMAN AND ROBIN* TONIGHT, OR I WOULD HAVE MADE *FONDUE.*
FORGIVE THE INTRUSION, MISS ALLISTER.
WE WANT TO ASK SOME QUESTIONS ABOUT *WAYLON JONES.*

CALL ME *EVA.* WE USED TO DATE. COME IN.

CAN I MAKE YOU MEN A DRINK?
OH, *UH*, GOLLY...
JUICE OR WATER WILL BE FINE, EVA. NOW, HAVE YOU HEARD FROM WAYLON RECENTLY?
NOPE. HE RAN OFF TO WORK WITH THAT *TUT* CHARACTER, HAVEN'T SEEN HIM SINCE.
FINE, I SAYS. BETTER OFF ALONE.

INTERESTING. YET I COULDN'T HELP BUT NOTICE...
...THE OTTOMAN IS PLACED FAR FROM THE LOUNGER, AS IF IT WERE PLACED BY SOMEONE WITH MUCH LONGER LEGS THAN YOU, MISS ALLISTER.
I WONDER IF I MIGHT HAVE A LOOK AROUND...
BE MY GUEST.

SMASH!!!
YAAH!!!

'EM,
BY!
HEY!
SPLUB

YOU CAPES AIN'T TAKIN' ME IN!
BRR-LONNNG
GIVE UP, WAYLON!

BOFF!

I AIN'T TWO-BIT ENFORCER WAYLON JONES ANYMORE...

...I'M KILLER CROC!!!

PSSSSSSKT

YAAAGHH!!
CRASH!

IT STINKS! IT *STINGS!*

THAT WAS THE CROCODILE REPELLENT YOU USED IN EGYPT!
YES, I WAS AFRAID IT WOULD BE NEEDED AGAIN.
THE ELIXIR JONES DRANK THERE HAS MADE HIM AS MUCH CROCODILE AS MAN.
LET ME GO!

THE POLICE WILL BE BY SOON TO PICK YOU UP, EVA-- FOR *ABETTING A FELON!*
THANKS FOR THE DRINK!

CROC CLEARLY WENT THIS WAY!
AFTER THIS BLOCK, IT DOESN'T LOOK LIKE HE LEFT AS MANY TRACES!

THINK, ROBIN. IF YOU WERE AS MUCH NILE CROCODILE AS MAN, WHAT WOULD YOUR INSTINCT BE NOW?
I'D HEAD TO...
...THE WATER!

EXACTLY! LOOK--NO MUNICIPAL ORKER WOULD HAVE LEFT THAT MANHOLE COVER OPEN LIKE THAT!

SOMETIMES OUR WAR ON CRIME TAKES US INTO THE DARKEST PLACES.
I'M READY IF YOU ARE, BATMAN.

EVA SPLASHED A LOT OF ALCOHOL ON ME--I HOPE IT DOESN'T IMPAIR MY JUDGMENT.
I'LL ASSURE CHIEF O'HARA THAT YOU DID NOT IMBIBE.

WOW... WE'RE IN HIS ELEMENT NOW!
WE MUST LURE HIM OUT, TAKE AWAY THE ELEMENT OF SURPRISE.

CROC! WE KNOW YOU'RE HERE, LET US HELP YOU!
I KNOW SCIENTISTS WHO MAY BE ABLE TO REVERSE YOUR CONDITION!

WHY WOULD I DO THAT? I'M THE TOUGHEST GUY IN GOTHAM, NOW!
YOU CAN EVEN EMPTY A GUN AT ME, AND THE BULLETS WILL BOUNCE OFF.

I NEVER USE GUNS.
STAY BACK, ROBIN, THIS IS BETWEEN ME... AND CROC.

HA!
THOOMP!

RRRH!!!

STAY STILL!
KRANG!!!

HOLY SPH CESSPOOLS--!
KLOCK!

GOTCHA!

YOU'RE DONE FOR!
UNH!
BATMAN!

YA CAN'T RUN AWAY NOW!
YA AIN'T A BAT, YOU'RE A HAMSTER!

HEY, WHAT GIVES!

KEEN!
ROBIN, GET TO THE OTHER SIDE OF THAT PIPE!

BA-WANNG!
YOW!

CLACK!
GOT HIM!

THE BAT-CUFFS CAN HOLD EVEN YOU, CROC!
OHHH... MY SKULL...
YOU SEE, OLD CHUM, BRAINS BEAT BRAWN!
NOW TO CALL THE COMMISSIONER TO SEND IN WILD ANIMAL SPECIALISTS.
AT LEAST I DON'T SMELL LIKE LIQUOR ANYMORE.

EMERGENCY BAT-TURN LEVER
ALL RED

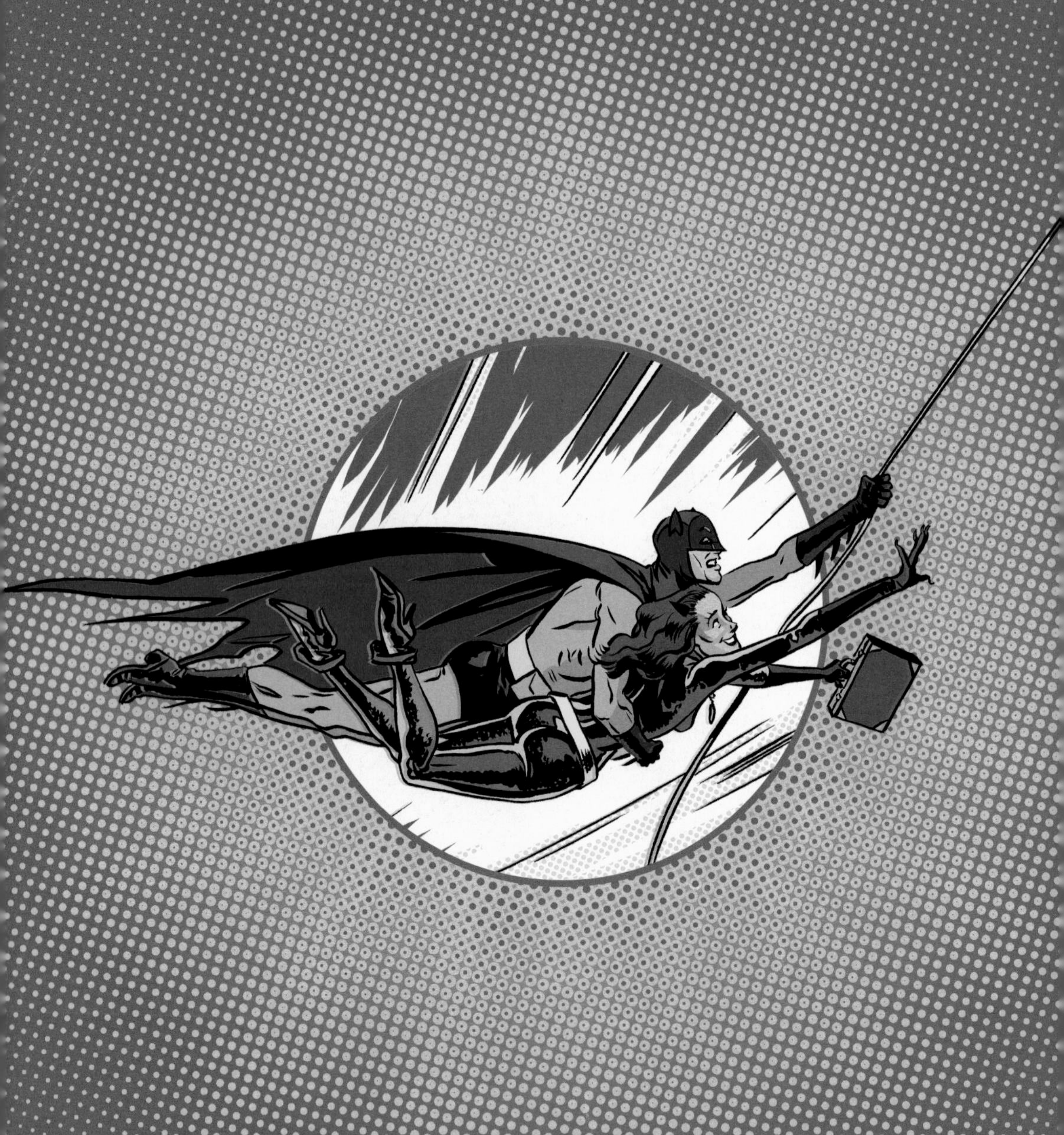

HAT'S
HIS?!
BRAKAKAKAAAKAKAKA
A SHOOT-OUT ON THE STREETS OF GOTHAM?
YOU'LL NEVER TAKE ME ALIVE, BAT-COPPERS!
HAHAHA HAAAA!
AIR 'EM OUT, MA!
HOLY HAIL OF BULLETS! MA PARKER MEANS BUSINESS!
SHE ALWAYS DOES, CHUM, BUT TODAY SHE SEEMS MORE UNHINGED THAN EVER BEFORE!
KAKAKA
BRAKABRAKA
“PARKER
REAKS OUT”
itten by JEFF PARKER Art by DEAN HASPIEL
y ALLEN PASSALAQUA Letters by WES ABBOTT
Cover by MICHAEL and LAURA ALLRED

AND HOW DID WE COME TO THIS, READERS? LOOK BACK TO EARLIER TODAY!
RIOT! AT THE WOMEN'S PRISON!
GOOD LUCK, CAPED CRUSADER!
I LIKE THEM LEGS, BOY WONDER! HAW, HAW!
THIS IS THE LAST OF 'EM.
GOSH!
THANKS FOR COMING OUT, DYNAMIC DUO, BUT AS YOU SEE, WE HAVE IT UNDER CONTROL, NOW.
INDEED, WARDEN.
STILL... COULD WE VISIT THE CELL OF THE MOTHERLY MOBSTER MA PARKER?

I CAN'T BELIEVE IT! HER DAUGHTER IS GONE, TOO!
SO LONG SUCKERS
HOW DID YOU KNOW, BATMAN?

RIOTS ARE A HALLMARK OF MA PARKER'S PRISON BEHAVIOR. SHE KNOWS BETTER THAN ANYONE HOW TO START ONE.
WE SENT HER HERE SIX MONTHS AGO. JUDGING BY THE SIZE OF THE PRISON GROUNDS, THAT WOULD BE ENOUGH TIME...

...TO DIG AN ESCAPE TUNNEL.
TUNNEL ON MY PR GROUND
SO LONG SUCKE
YEP! WE WENT THIS WA

WARDEN, WE HAVE TO RACE TO THE MEN'S PENITENTIARY! I'D ADVISE YOU TO CHECK THE CELLS AND MAKE SURE NO ONE ELSE FOLLOWED THE PARKERS.
IT SEEMS UNLIKELY, BUT I GUESS ANYTHING'S POSSIBLE, ISN'T IT, BATMAN?
WHY ARE WE GOING TO THE OTHER STATE PEN?
REMEMBER, LAD, THE OTHER THING MA VALUES AS MUCH AS MONEY...
...FAMILY! HER FIRST DESIRE WOULD BE TO BREAK HER SONS OUT OF PRISON, TOO.
"SHE MAY HAVE BEEN PLANNING THIS PART FOR MONTHS."
VISITATION
NEXT!
STATE THE REASON FOR YOUR VISIT.
EH? OH, HEH HEH. IT'S M'BOY'S BIRTHDAY.
OH, COME ON, LADY, A CAKE? WHAT, IS IT FULL OF FILES AND KEYS?
OH HO HO HO! OH, MY, NO, IT'S DEVIL'S FOOD.
I'M GONNA HAVE TO INSPECT IT.
GO AHEAD, SONNY...
...TAKE A GOOD LOOK!
SOCKO!

FFSSST
BRRRRRINGGRRRRRNGRRRNGG
HA! WHO ELSE WOULD BREAK OUTTA ONE PRISON AND GO RIGHT TO ANOTHER? MA, YOU'RE A MESS!
I KNOW IT! GO GET THE CAR READY, GIRL.
PRETTY BOY! MAD DOG! RISE AND SHINE, SWEETHEARTS!
MA!
HOT DOG, WE'RE FREE!
MA PARKER! WHAT ABOUT US?
I ALWAYS THOUGHT OF YA AS, LIKE, ME MUDDER!
GRUNDY COULD BE ZOMBIE SON!
YA WOULDN'T LEAVE A FELLOW KILLER IN MOTHBALLS, WOULD YA?
OKAY, BUT HERE'S THE DEAL, AND NO ONE CROSSES MA PARKER.
I'LL BREAK YOU OUT...BUT Y HAVE TO STEAL FORWARD!

BAM!
OFF!
THAT'S ALL YOU WANTED US TO DO? YOU KNOW WE'D DO THAT ANYWAY, RIGHT?
BUT YOU WOULDN'T DO IT TOGETHER, MOTH. THAT'S THE KEY.
UST WANT YBODY TO THE VALUE FAMILY.
UGH!
SURRENDER, MA PARKER!
WE'VE LOWERED THE STEEL BARRIERS TO THE ENTRANCES--
--YOU'LL NEVER GET THROUGH!
OH, PSHAW! THESE PEOPLE ARE SO IGNORANT.
MAMAS THINK OF EVERYTHING.

KABLOOEY!
OH, MA!
YIPPEEE!
WE NEED SOME BANJO MUSIC--
STEP ON IT, LEGS!
VRRRMMMM!!!
HOW MANY SQUAD CARS ARE COMIN', MA?
IT AIN'T JOHN LAW!
IT'S JOHN BAT!
HANG ON, BOYS, I GOT PRESENTS IN HERE FOR YA.

AW, MA, YOU REMEMBERED WHAT I LIKE!
GO ON, HONEY, TEST IT OUT...ON THAT *BATMOBILE.*
TOMMY GUNS!
CLOSING THE BULLETPROOF CANOPY.
HMMMMMMMMMMMMMMM
THE BAT-GLASS IS...HOLDING... SO FAR...
STAY CALM, ROBIN.
BRAKAKAKAA
I CAN'T STAND BULLETPROOF CARS!
MAMA! WHAT ARE YOU DOING?
I'M GONNA BUST THEM *OUTTA* THERE!
MA, *PLEASE!* GET BACK IN THE CAR, THIS IS *EXTREMELY DANGEROUS!*

NO!
MY BABIES!
YAAAH!
MAAAA!

SPLOOSH!
LEGS AND MAD DOG CAN'T SWIM-- WHY DIDN'T I EVER TEACH THEM?

ROBIN, CUFF PRETTY BOY WHEN HE REACHES THE SHORE!
I'LL BRING THE OTHER TWO UP--
NOT WITHOUT ME!
THOSE ARE MY LITTLE DARLINGS!

SPLOOSH!

ROBIN! WHAT HAPPENED?
THEY'VE BEEN DOWN A LONG TIME, WARDEN.
BUT IF ANYONE CAN BRING THEM BACK, IT'S...

...BATMAN!
IT ALMOST TOOK TOO LONG, BUT MA'S HELP MADE THE DIFFERENCE.
COFF! SPUT!

MA'S TOO CRAZY, I WON'T TAKE HER BACK! SHE TURNED MY PRISON INTO MAYHEM!
AND NEARLY DESTROYED MINE!
I WOULD LIKE TO PROPOSE A SOLUTION...

THE ARKHAM INSTITUTE FOR THE CRIMINALLY INSANE...
YOUR RECOMMENDATION WORKED, BATMAN.
SINCE WE PUT MA AND HER CHILDREN TOGETHER HERE AT ARKHAM, THEY'VE BEEN CALM AND EASY TO MANAGE.
Home Sweet Home!

I'M PLEASED, DR. HUGO.
BUT I HAVE TO WONDER NOW...
"...IF THIS WASN'T HER REAL PLAN ALL ALONG?"
...THE CITY RESTS AT EASE WITH THE PARKER GANG UNDER LOCK AND KEY AGAIN...

...BUT BOTH WARDENS REPORT THAT THERE ARE FOUR MAJOR VILLAINS AT LARGE IN THE WAKE OF THE PRISON BREAK!
I DON'T KNOW WHO THE OTHER THREE ARE, BUT THE MAJOR ONE IS
ME-RROWW!
NOW TO MAKE UP FOR LOST TIME!
WHAT'S CATWOMAN UP TO?
READ ON, BAT-FAN!

OK LIVELY, GOTHAM CITY! MANHUNT LIKE NO OTHER IS UNDERWAY!
THE EAST END IS ALL CLEAR, ROBIN!
WE'VE COVERED A LOT OF GROUND NOW THAT YOU CAN RIDE THE BATCYCLE.
WE SURE HAVE! WITH THE CRIME LOCALES THAT THE BAT-COMPUTER GUESSED, WE'LL FIND THE ESCAPED CONVICTS IN NO TIME!
TOING!
SPROING!
RIGHTER THAN YOU KNOW, CRIME-FINDERS.
WITH DANGEROUS VILLAINS AT LARGE, SPLITTING UP YOUR SEARCHES WAS THE RIGHT MOVE.
BUT I'M GUESSING BATMAN MEANT FOR YOU TO FIND US AND CONTACT HIM BEFORE MAKING CONTACT.
SEE, ANTICIPATING BATMAN AND ACTING FIRST IS THE M.O.* OF KILLER MOTH.
AND CATCHIN' PUNKS IS THE B-O OF KILLER CROC!
AND... AND... AND SOLOMON GRUNDY!
OH NO!!!
*MODUS OPERANDI (METHOD OF OPERATING).

ACROSS THE CITY...
MY TIARA!!! THE SIAMESE SAPPHIRE IS GONE!
HEH, YOU SHOULDN'T OWN JEWELS THAT SOUND LIKE CATS, RICH LADY.
JUST AS THE BAT-COMPUTER GUESSED YOU WOULD SEEK OUT, CATWOMAN!
BATMAN! I'VE ONLY BEEN OUT OF THE PEN FOR FOUR DAYS, YOU COULD GIVE ME A LITTLE MORE TIME.
YOU MEAN MORE TIME FOR CRIME!
YES! YOU GET ME!
I ALWAYS SUSPECTED YOU DI --AH!!
THIS IS IT!

MY... HERO!
NOT TODAY.
I SHOULD HAVE KNOWN YOU WOULDN'T MAKE ME USE UP ONE OF MY NINE LIVES.
AH... WELL, LIFE IS PRECIOUS AND WE ALL DO WHAT WE MUST...!
AHEM-- NOW LET'S RETURN THAT TIARA.
THE LADY ASKED FOR MY AUTOGRAPH, SHE COULDN'T HAVE BEEN TOO WORRIED ABOUT IT--
BATMAN, BATMAN!
THEY GOT BATGIRL... AND ROBIN!
KIDS, ALWAYS TALKING ABOUT NONSENSE.
WHO GOT THEM?
SOME REALLY BIG GUYS! ONE HAD CHALKY SKIN... AND THE OTHER LOOKED LIKE A REPTILE!
SOLOMON GRUNDY AND KILLER CROC!
AND SOME OTHER GUY WITH ANTENNAS LIKE A BUG--
OH, KILLER MOTH, NATCH.

THEY'LL USE BATGIRL AND ROBIN AS A TRAP FOR *ME*, THEY'RE IN TERRIBLE DANGER.
I CAN'T SPARE EVEN A *SECOND* TO TAKE YOU TO THE POLICE--THOSE MEN ARE DEADLY!
OHHHH... I CAN'T BELIEVE I'M GOING TO DO THIS...

THEN DON'T TAKE ME IN. *LET'S GO.*
I CALL *SHOTGUN.*
WH-WHAT?

LIKE YOU SAY, THOSE THREE ARE NOTHING TO SNEEZE AT, AND YOU NEED HELP.
TONIGHT, I'M YOUR ASSISTANT.
...

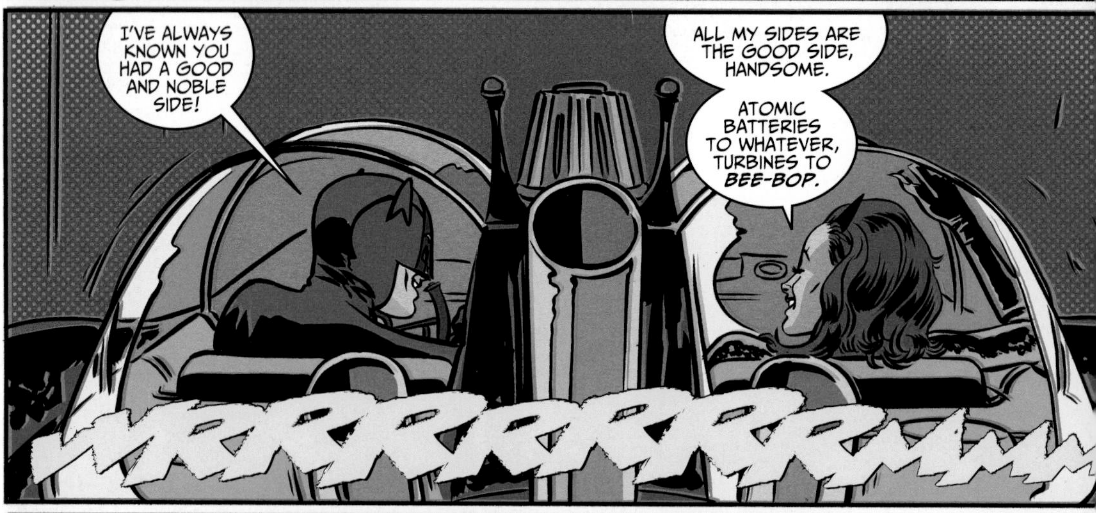
I'VE ALWAYS KNOWN YOU HAD A GOOD AND NOBLE SIDE!
ALL MY SIDES ARE THE GOOD SIDE, HANDSOME.
ATOMIC BATTERIES TO WHATEVER, TURBINES TO *BEE-BOP.*
VRRRRRRRRRMMM

SKRRRRRRR!!!
HEAD TO THE *WHARF*, I HAVE A NOTION THEY'RE NEAR THE OCEAN. I KNOW *EVERYONE'S* HIDEOUTS.

EVERYONE COMFORTABLE UP THERE?
I TOOK YOUR UTILITY BELTS SO YOU CAN BE EXTRA-RELAXED.
AND COMING UP SOON WILL BE THE REFRESHING DUNK!
TOO BAD YOUR LITTLE SHARK-REPELLANT SPRAYS ARE IN THESE BELTS.
GOSH!
YOU CAN SAY THAT AGAIN.
WHMMMMMMMM
LOWER BAIT SO CAN CATCH SHARK! GRUNDY HUNGRY!
HANG ON, SOL! YOU'RE SENDING THE BOAT OUT!
AND THE BAIT IS REALLY FOR BATMAN, SEE?
I HAVE TO BROADCAST THIS AS FOOTAGE, PUT OUT A TRAIL OF PAPER MOTHS, AND LEAD HIM INTO THE BIG NET.
THEN WE'LL DROWN THEM ALL, AND SURE, IF IT CATCHES ANY SEAFOOD, IT'S ALL YOURS, BIG GUY.
I'M SORRY, MOTH, BUT I'M ON A BUSY SCHEDULE.
MIND IF WE START EARLIER?
OH, GOOD!

IT'S ONLY THREE TO ONE, THIS SHOULD BE EASY.
I'LL SHOW YA EASY, BATS!
GRUNDY CRUSH BATMAN!
HE HAS NOWHERE TO GO UP THERE, THE FOOL--WE'VE GOT HIM!
SOMETIMES THE ELEMENT OF SURPRISE IS OVERRATED, BATMAN.
YES, MOTH...
...BUT DISTRACTION IS INVALUABLE.
CATWOMAN!?!
LOOK BACK DOWN, BOYS.
THANKS, BATMAN!
I CAN'T BELIEVE IT--CATWOMAN HELPED YOU?
NEVER UNDERESTIMATE THE POTENTIAL FOR GOODNESS IN PEOPLE'S HEARTS, BATGIRL.

THOK!
I LIKE TO HEAR HIM TALK ABOUT MY HEART, BUT MY FEET ARE WHERE IT'S AT!
NGH!
I CALL THIS DANCE THE ZOMBIE STOMP!
RAHR!!!
WOW, CATWOMAN IS PRETTY GOOD IN A FIGHT AGAINST BAD GUYS!
EXCEPT IT DOESN'T USUALLY BENEFIT US, BOY WONDER!
COULD IT BE SHE'S ALWAYS BEEN... HOLDING BACK?
BECAUSE SHE DIDN'T REALLY WANT TO HURT ME?
HAVE I PERHAPS ALSO DONE THE SAME?

THAT WOULD MEAN THAT I LO--
AH!
PAY ATTENTION, BAT-BUM!

NOW!
NGH!
HA HA! LOOKIT THE KIDS TRYIN' TO FIGHT HEAVYWEIGHT!

PFFT. STEP ASIDE-- LET A WOMAN DEAL WITH THIS.

HEY, TALL, PALE AND UGLY, MIND IF I KNOCK YOU DOWN AGAIN?
GRUNDY CRUSH CAT LADY!

HAH. YOU DON'T HAVE ENOUGH BRAIN CELLS TO AIM STRAIGHT.
ME SHOW YOU!

KAPOW!!
AND THAT IS HOW YOU MANIPULATE A MAN!
WELL, DEAD MAN, SAME DIFF.
WE'VE GOT KILLER MOTH!
SHINING A LIGHT IN MY EYE WAS A CHEAP TRICK!
BUT HOW CAN WE BRING DOWN GRUNDY?
HUMAN STRENGTH IS NOT ENOUGH AGAINST HIM!
BUT THIS WINCH PULLS UP A TON AT A TIME.
AND IT CAN THROW A CATCH OUT, TOO!
KWHAM!
WHRAAAH!!!

HE'S DOWN THERE WITH THE SHARKS!
POOR SHARKS!
HE CAN'T DROWN, HE'LL WANDER AROUND ON THE OCEAN FLOOR.
HOPEFULLY HEADING AWAY FROM LAND. BUT...
...IT APPEARS CATWOMAN SNUCK AWAY IN THE ACTION.
STILL A CRIMINAL, AT HER CORE.
DON'T BE SO QUICK TO JUDGE, BATGIRL. IMAGINE IF ANY OF US HAD VERY DIFFERENT CIRCUMSTANCES IN OUR PASTS.
GOSH.
I WON'T SOON FORGET THAT WHEN WE TRULY NEEDED HER HELP, SHE WAS THERE FOR ME...I MEAN, US.
AW.
OKRA
"CATWOMAN COMES ABOUT!"
Written by JEFF PARKER
Art and Colors by JONATHAN CASE
Letters by WES ABBOTT

COMPLETE SET OF CRIME FIGHTING EQUIPMENT
LIFE
BATMAN
CHARTER MEMBER
Batman & Robin Society
THE BOY WONDER

KA-RASH!

GOTHAM CITY POLICE
ANOTHER QUIET DAY IN GOTHAM CITY.
"MAIN TITLE"
Written by LEE ALLRED
Art and Cover by MICHAEL and LAURA ALLRED
Letters by WES ABBOTT
PERHAPS TOO QUIET.

NOT A CRIMINAL IS STIRRING.
NOT EVEN A LOUSE.
ZZZZZZZZ

GOTHAM'S ENTIRE CRIMINAL ELEMENT HAS JUST UP AND VANISHED!
AYE. WHAT CAN THE DIVVELS BE UP TO?

MEYBBE WE SHOULD--
AND SAY WHAT? THAT LAW AND ORDER HAVE BROKEN OUT ALL OVER GOTHAM?

MEANWHILE, ON A MOVIE STUDIO BACKLOT IN THE HEART OF GOTHAM.
GOTHAM STUDIOS
WAUGH
I'VE ALWAYS SAID CRIME IS A BUSINESS, AND EVERY BUSINESS NEEDS ITS BUSINESS CONVENTIONS.
AND IT'S ALL TAX DEDUCTIBLE!
WAUGH WAUGH WAUGH
SULFURIC ACID
HUMAN KEY DUPLICATOR
PAT. PENDING

THE PURRRRFECT VENUE.
WHAT BETTER PLACE TO HIDE ROBBERS, RASCALS, REPROBATE AND RAPSCALLIONS BUT A MOVIE STUDIO?
FEED PAPER IN HERE
VOLUME CONTROL
DANGER

WHO'D BOTHER TO LOOK FOR CROOKS HERE? WHO COULD TELL?
HOOHOO HOOOO!
JUST MAKE SURE THIS DOESN'T END UP A CAT-ASTROPHE LIKE OUR LAST JOINT ENDEAVOR.
WAUGH
ABSOLUTELY. THIS TIME, NO SUBMARINES! NO COMMODORES!
WAUGH
BAT-SHARK REPELLENT! OUGHTA BE A LAW...
AH, THE TRAINING WORKSHOPS ARE RUNNING LIKE CLOCKWORK...
THIS IS MY COS-TUME, THIS IS MY GUN!
LOUDER, LADIES!!!
DRILL SGT
WORKSHOP: BASICS FOR BADGUYS
DON'T LEAVE THE ROOM 'TIL THE DEATHTRAP IS DONE!
AND OUR BREAKOUT PANELS ARE DOING FINE, ALL THINGS CONSIDERED.
NO, NO, NO, GRUNDY! THE FILE GOES INSIDE THE CAKE. INSIDE THE CAKE!
BREAKOUT PANEL: GETAWAY GENIUS
YOU SUCH GETAWAY GENIUS, WHY NOT JUST STAY OUT OF JAIL IN FIRST PLACE?
BOSS! BOSS! WE GOT A PROBLEM!
DON'T TELL ME THE CAPED CRUSADERS HAVE ALREADY--!

NOT THEM, BOSS. IT'S KING COBRA.
HE CAME IN COSTUME LIKE YOUSE GUYS SAID NOT TO DO SO AS NOT TO DRAW ATTENTION.
WE CAN'T PULL HIS MASK OFF, NEITHER--
--NO MATTER HOW HARD WE TRY!
HEEHEE! FORGOT TO MENTION--I GAVE KING COBRA SPECIAL MASK PERMISSION.
LITTLE MISHAP WITH BAT-GLUE LAST TIME OUT.
HA HA HA!
THAT'S ALL FELINELY DIVINE, BUT WHA ABOUT ATTENDANCE FIGURES? ARE W AT LEAST BREAKING EVEN?
BETTER'N EXPECTED, BOSS. I GO DA NUMBERS RIGHT HERE.
...WE GOT EVERY GOTHAM SUPER-CROOK HERE, FROM ATOMIC MAN TO ZEBRA-MAN!
WHY, ATOM MASTER! IT'S BEEN AGES! HOW'S MRS. MASTER AND ALL THE LITTLE ATOMS?
AND SIGNALMAN! CUNNINGLY DISGUISED AS AN ACTUAL RAILROAD SIGNALMAN, I SEE!
WE ONLY GOTS ONE MAJOR NO-SHOW--THE RIDDLER.
BAH! WE DIDN'T INVITE HIM! NOT AFTER LAST TIME!
HISSSSSSS!
WAUGH
HIM AND HIS COCKAMAMIE RIDDLES!
WAUGH
OUGHTA BE A LAW...

WHILE AT GOTHAM STATE PENITENTIARY, THE PLOT THICKENS--
"NO SOAP, BOSS!
I DONE LIKE YOU SAID. I TALK TO PENGUIN, I TALK TO CATWOMAN, I EVEN TALK TO JOKER-- WHICH IS NO TREAT, LET ME TELL YOU!
THEY ALL REFUSED-- AN' WIT' EXTREME PREJUDICE!--A LET YOU ATTEND THEIR LITTLE CONFAB.

THEY TELL ME YOU MIGHT AS WELL BE WORKING FOR BATMAN, YOU AND YOUR RIDDLES.
I DO NOT THINK THEY LIKES YOU NONE, BOSS.

THEY
DARE
BLACKBALL
ME?
ME?!?

RIDDLE ME THIS--WHY IS REVENGE LIKE A BOWL OF ICE CREAM? BECAUSE IT'S A DISH BEST SERVED COLD!
I HAVE A LITTLE DELIVERY FOR YOU TO MAKE, JIGSAW...

STATELY WAYNE MANOR.
GOSH, BRUCE. IT'S TOO QUIET! IF WE DON'T GET SOME BAT-ACTION SOON--!!!
STEADY, OLD CHUM. REMEMBER OUR ULTIMATE BAT-GOAL IS A CRIME-FREE GOTHAM.
WE SHOULD BE GLAD THINGS ARE QUIET, NOT CRAVING "ACTION," AS YOU PUT IT.
AS SOCRATES ONCE SAID--
SIR, A =AHEM!= TELEPHONE CALL FOR YOU AND MASTER DICK.
A BOX OF FILM REELS WITH RIDDLES TAPED TO THEM?
WE'LL BE RIGHT THERE, COMMISSIONER.
BRUCE
GOSH! AND I THOUGHT THE RIDDLER WAS STILL IN JAIL.
DICK
BRUCE

ATOMIC BATTERIES TO POWER!
EMERGENCY BAT TURN LEVER
TURBINES TO SPEED!
KOFF KOFF
WHOOOSH!!!
ROGER. READY TO MOVE OUT.
2F-3567
GOTHAM 1966
WHOOOSH!!!
SSSSQUEAL!
SLIDE!

KRROOOOMM!!
Gotham City
14 MILES

--BUT WHY WOULD THE RIDDLER SEND RIDDLES TO HELP US, CAPED CRUSADER?
I SUSPECT A FALLING-OUT, COMMISSIONER. AS THE OLD TRUISM SAYS, THERE IS NO HONOR AMONG THIEVES.
A THOUGHT, PERHAPS, TO CONSIDER BEFORE TAKING UP A LIFE OF CRIME.
"WHEN IS A TOKYO TRAFFIC LIGHT UNHAPPY?"
WHEN IT'S GREEN.
IN JAPAN, A GO LIGHT IS AOI, A JAPANESE WORD MEANING GREEN OR BLUE.
"WHEN IS THINKING LIKE A BUNCH OF OUT-OF-TOWN SHRINERS?"
TOO EASY, BATMAN! WHEN IT'S CONVENTIONAL!
AYE, AND MAYBE SO, BOY WONDER, BUT FER THE LIFE O' ME, I CAN'T PIECE IT TOGETHER.
ALL TOO OBVIOUS, CHIEF O'HARA. A SOLUTION THAT PRESAGES SUCH A DIRE AND INSIDIOUS CALAMITY, I SCARCE IMAGINE IT POSSIBLE.
THE REASON FOR GOTHAM'S CURRENT PRETERNATURAL CALM IS THAT GOTHAM'S VILLAINRY IS ALL GATHERED FOR A CROOK CONVENTION HELD AT THE OLD GREENE-WAY FILM STUDIOS!
TO THE BATMOBILE, ROBIN!
SURE AND BEGORRA! HERE WE PUZZLE OVER THEM TRICKY RIDDLES FER HOURS, AND THEM BE SOLVING IT IN FIFTEEN SECONDS FLAT.
WHAT WOULD WE EVER DO WITHOUT THEM, CHIEF? WHAT, INDEED.

WE'LL
CLIMB UP THE
ENE-WAY STUDIO
FFICE BUILDING
: A GOOD LOOK
VER THE MOVIE
LOT.
STAND BACK FOR BATARANG TOSS, ROBIN!
GOSH, BATMAN! I THOUGHT THIS STUDIO WAS ABANDONED, BUT THIS MAIN OFFICE IS CRAWLING WITH PEOPLE.

NOT PEOPLE, ROBIN, REPORTERS. TONIGHT'S THE PRESS CONFERENCE ANNOUNCING THE STUDIO'S SALE TO THE GOTHAM BROTHERS CONGLOMERATE.
THE AUDACITY OF THOSE FIENDS HIDING RIGHT UNDER THE NOSE OF THE PRESS!
GREAT CAESAR'S GHOST! IT'S BATMAN!

WE'RE FROM THE DAILY PLANET.
ANYTHING WE CAN DO TO AID YOU, CAPED CRUSADER?
JUST CONTINUE DELIVERING NEWS ACCURATELY AND IN AN IMPARTIAL AND UNBIASED MANNER, GOOD CITIZEN.
REMEMBER! A REPORTER'S JOB IS TO REPORT EVENTS, NOT INFLUENCE THEM!

WELL SAID, BOY WONDER!
GEE! BATMAN!
TOO BAD CLARK HAD TO STAY BACK IN METROPOLIS TO COVER ANOTHER STORY.

SO WHAT ARE WE LOOKING FOR UP HERE ANYWAY, BATMAN?
A PLACE TO PARK THE BATMOBILE, OLD CHUM. THE PERFECT PLACE...
HUH?!?

AH, HA! SO THAT'S HOW THEY SNUCK IN EN MASSE! HOW UTTERLY SIMPLE AND YET SO DIABOLICAL!
SEE THERE? THAT MAN TAKING A SMOKE BREAK OUTSIDE SOUNDSTAGE 54?
IT'S OUR OLD PAL--BUT WITHOUT HIS COSTUME.
HOLY 20TH CENTURY! FOX OF THE TERRIBLE TRIO!
I'M TERRIBLE AT FACES, BUT I NEVER FORGET A MASK!

HE'S DISCONNECTED THE EMERGENCY FIRE DOOR ALARM IN ORDER TO SNEAK OUT FOR A SMOKE.
IRONIC THAT A "COFFIN NAIL" SHOULD PUT THE NAIL IN HIS COFFIN.
WE'LL ENTER THROUGH THAT SAME ALARM-LESS DOOR.

BUT FIRST, TO PARK THE BATMOBILE BY REMOTE BAT-CONTROL FOR A LITTLE BAT-SURPRISE OF OUR OWN...
HAS BATMAN GOT THE DROP ON DOZENS OF DIABOLIC DO-BADDERS?
OR IS HE UNKNOWINGLY A BAT-CHUMP IN THEIR CLEVER, CONNIVING TRAP?

DE THE CROOK CONVENTION, VILLAINS ARE ONTO BATMAN'S ALTHY ARRIVAL, R SHORT UTES AGO...
JOKER! MY SECURITY CAMERAS HAVE PICKED UP BATMAN AND ROBIN DRIVING UP IN THE BATMOBILE.
GOOD WORK, MISTER CAMERA!

FOX, SHARK AND VULTURE! YOU'VE BEEN PROMOTED TO DECOYS!
LURE THAT BAT-BRAIN INSIDE THE FIRE DOOR. DON'T LET ON THAT WE KNOW HE'S HERE.

CLAYFACE! TIME FOR A LITTLE GREEN-SCREEN MOVIE MAGIC.
SIGNALMAN, MILO, CATMAN, DEADSHOT AND KING COBRA! YOU BACK HIM UP!

MERE MOMENTS LATER...
GOSH, BATMAN! THIS REEN CORRIDOR! CAN'T TELL FLOOR, WALL OR CEILING APART!
IT'S USED FOR CHROMA KEY FILMING--GREEN-SCREENING--A TECHNIQUE WHERE A SPECIFIC COLOR DOESN'T REGISTER VISIBLY ON FILM.

ODD. AS ANY STUDENT OF FILMOGRAPHY WOULD KNOW, A "GREEN SCREEN" IS ACTUALLY BLUE, BUT THIS ROOM--
HOLY MIDORI, BATMAN! JUST LIKE THAT JAPANESE TRAFFIC LIGHT RIDDLE.
EXACTLY, OLD CHUM! BUT FOR NOW, THE TERRIBLE TRIO--JUST AHEAD!

SOCKS ON FOX, FOX!
SOCK!
YOU'VE LAID
POW!
NO REMORSE FOR A REMORA LIKE YOU, SHARK!
ZOK!
THAT'S THREE DOWN...
...AND THREE HUNDRED TO GO. BUT A GOOD BEGINNING, NONETHELESS.

TO THE MAIN HALL!
MAIN HAUL IS RIGHT!
UM, IS IT JUST ME, OR ARE THE WALLS MELTING LIKE CLAY?

LIKE CLAYFACE, YOU MEAN!

READY, OLD CHUM?
ONE, TWO--

NOW!
POW
DIF!
BAM
SOK!
BLAP!

WAUGH
SO MUCH FOR YOUR FOOLPROOF AMBUSH, JOKER!
WAUGH
PSHAW! IT WAS A GOOD PLAN. JUST A POOR CHOICE OF LACKEYS.
GREAT! JUST LIKE LAST TIME! A PURR-FECT FIASCO!

WAUGH
THERE ARE THREE HUNDRED OF US! THEY CAN'T BEAT US ALL!
WAUGH
BAT-VILLAINS! ATTACK!!!

US AGAINST ONLY THREE HUNDRED? YOU'D THINK THE PENGUIN WOULD WANT BETTER ODDS.

I CALL DIBS ON EGGHEAD! I STILL OWE HIM FOR THAT EGG SHAMPOO!

SPLAT THE BAT TO THE MAT!

THEN SHOOT 'EM WITH YOUR GA
RAT-A-TAT-TAT!

OUR BELEAGUERED BAT-HEROES BATTLE BRAVELY...
BIFF!
OOOOF!
BOP

POP
...BUT FOR HOW LONG?!?
WHIZ

WHERE'D YOU GET YOUR THUGS, PENGUIN? GLASS JAWS "R" US?
HEY! I RESEMBLE THAT REMARK!
WILD!

UGH!

OOF!

PACE YOURSELF, ROBIN.
HOLY SISYPHUS! THEY JUST KEEP COMING!

MEEOW-OWCH!
BY THE TIME WE'VE PUNCHED ALL OF THEM OUT ONCE--

--THE FIRST ONES ARE BACK FOR SECONDS!
OOF!

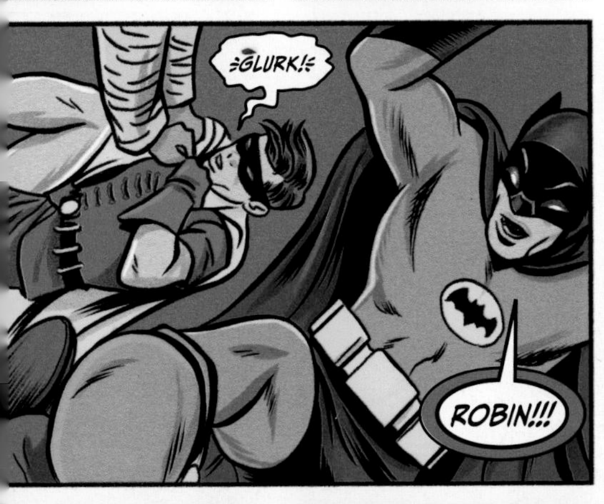
GLURK!
ROBIN!!!

WE GOT 'EM ON THE RUN NOW, BOYS!
IF YOU SO MUCH AS TOUCH ONE HAIR ON THAT BOY'S HEAD--

WHO'S TOUCHING? WHO'S TOUCHING?

WILD!
WOULD YOU STOP--?! GAD, THAT'S ANNOYING!

I'D LIKE TO PAUSE FOR STATION IDENTIFICATION!

THEY'RE WEAKENING! POUR IT ON!
JUST--
--TOO--
--MANY--!

DOGPILE!!!
HOLY NO FAIR!

GE-RON-I-MO!!
GE-RON-I-MEE
DON'T--
--GIVE--
--UP--

--JUST YET.
IF I CAN JUST-- JUST--

--REACH REMOTE--
--CONTROL BUTTON--
CLICK!

UH-OH.
I DISTINCTLY HEARD A CLICK.
I HATE IT WHEN HIS UTILITY BELT CLICKS. SOMETHING BAD ALWAYS HAPPENS WHEN HIS UTILITY BELT CLICKS.

BEEP
ATOMIC-BATTERIES-TO-POWER.
BEEP
TURBINES-TO-SPEED.
BEEP
READY-TO-MOVE-OUT!

BEEP
TARGET-ACQUIRED. ROUTE-SET.

BEEP
MAXIMUM-ACCELERATION-ACHIEVED.

BEEP
BAT-BATTERING-RAM-DEPLOYED.

BEEP
BAT-BEAM-EXTENDED.

BEEP
BAT-BEAM-NOW-ON-LINE.
BEEP
TARGET-ACQUIRED.

KA-RASH!
ZZZZAAPP!
HOLY UNSAFE AT ANY SPEED!
NO FAIR! WE WERE WINNING!
VEHICULAR MANSLAUGHTER! SUCH A LAWSUIT I'LL SLAP ON YOU!
SOME DAYS YOU GET THE BARRIS AND SOME DAYS THE BARRIS GETS YOU!
A-ANYBODY G-GET THE LICENSE NUMBER OF THAT BAT-TRUCK?
2F-3587? TP-6597? I CAN'T TELL-- I'M SEEING DOUBLE...
RIDDLE ME THIS, MY BACKSTABBING PEERS--
--WHY IS A RIDDLER SCORNED LIKE A CURATE'S EGG?
BECAUSE HE'S GOOD IN PARTS!
GET IT? HELPING THE GOOD GUYS? GOOD IN PARTS?
GROAN
NOT THAT OLD APOPHTHEGM!

MERINGUE!
STOMPY-BOOT!
WADDLE-KICK!
OH, SHUT UP!

'M THINKING
V WOULD BE A
PURRRFECT
TIME TO--
--CATFOOT IT OUT OF HERE? NEVER SAW THAT ONE COMING!
WAUGH
EXIT, STAGE RIGHT!
WAUGH

QUIET, YOU ANTARCTIC ABERRATION! YOU WADDLE TOO LOUD.
WE'RE GOING TO MAKE IT, WE'RE GOING TO MAKE IT, WE'RE GOING TO MAKE--

IS THIS A
RIVATE PARTY,
R CAN ANYONE
JOIN IN?
WAUGH
WHO'S NEXT? BAT-DOG? MAYBE BAT-HORSE?

SAW YOUR BATMOBILE DRIVING ITSELF AND THOUGHT YOU MIGHT NEED SOME HELP.
FROM YOU, ANY BAT-TIME, ANY BAT-CAPER!

POLICE SIRENS!
THEY FOLLOWED ME IN. AND A BUNCH OF THOSE REPORTERS, TOO!

SMILE FOR THE BIRDIE, MISTER CAMERA!
GOOD ONE, PETEY!
AMATEURS! YOUR FOCAL STOPS ARE ALL WRONG!
PLEASE, PLEASE! GENTLEMEN AND LADIES OF THE PRESS!
WE'RE MERELY CONCERNED CITIZE DOING WHAT WE CAN.
OUR WORK WOULD BE IN VAIN WITHOUT ALL OF YO GOING PEACEFULLY ABO YOUR LIVES, PEACEFULL OBEYING THE LAW, AND DOING YOUR CIVIC DUTY.
BATMAN! BATMAN! VICKI VALE, GOTHAM GAZETTE--
--CLARK KENT, DAILY--
--SENTINEL, RITT BRIED REPORTING--
--JACK RYDER--
--RADIO STATION WHIZ-- JEEPERS, QUIT SHOVING!
--NELLIE MAJORS, GOTHAM CITY HERALD--
NOW, IF YOU'LL EXCUSE US--
--WE SEEM TO BE NEEDED ELSEWHERE IN OUR NEVER-ENDING BATTLE AGAINST THE FORCES OF CRIME AND EVIL! MAY WE MEET AGAIN!
TO THE BATMOBILE, ROBIN!

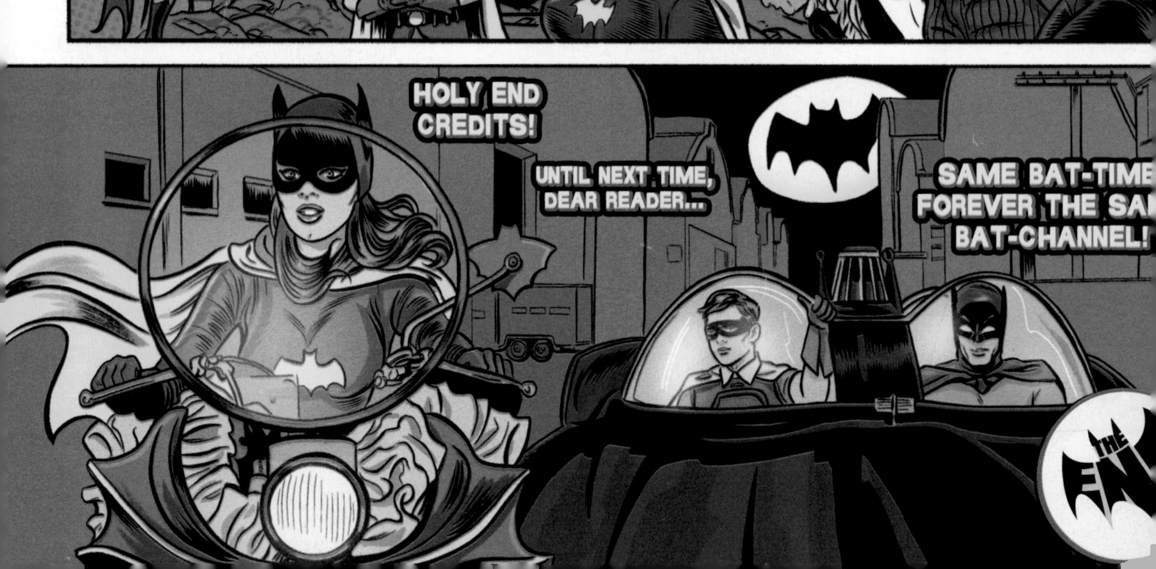
HOLY END CREDITS!
UNTIL NEXT TIME, DEAR READER...
SAME BAT-TIME FOREVER THE SA BAT-CHANNEL!
THE EN

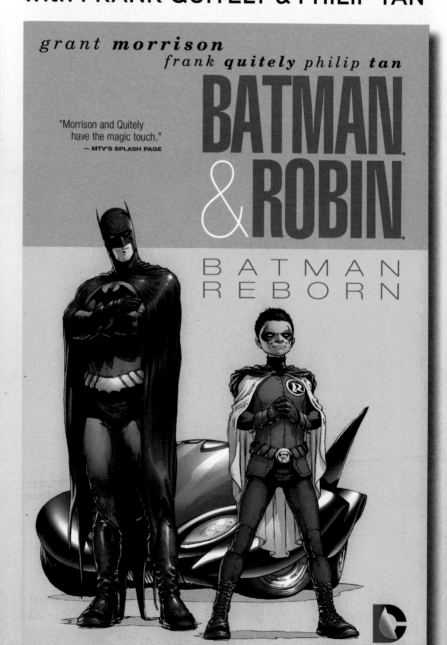

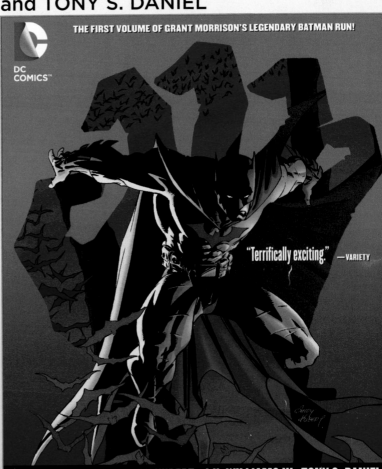